## "How certain are you the child is mine?"

"One hundred percent positive. You're the only man I've been with in six years."

Something dark sparked in his eyes.

His cold gaze didn't leave hers. He was weighing her up, she realized.

All she could do was stare back and hope he recognized the truth in her eyes. If he chose not to believe her...

Her whole body trembled. She knew what the consequences would be if he decided her claims of his paternity were a lie—destitution until the baby was born...

Still staring intently at her, he took a long drink of his coffee before placing the cup down on the small round table to the side of his chair. "If you are telling the truth then answer me this," he said in a low growl. "If I am the father of your child, what in hell gave you the right to hide it from me?"

**Michelle Smart**'s love affair with books started when she was a baby and would cuddle them in her cot. A voracious reader of all genres, she found her love of romance established when she stumbled across her first Harlequin book at the age of twelve. She's been reading them—and writing them—ever since. Michelle lives in Northamptonshire, England, with her husband and two young Smarties.

### Books by Michelle Smart

### Harlequin Presents

*Stranded with Her Greek Husband*
*Claiming His Baby at the Altar*
*Innocent's Wedding Day with the Italian*

### A Billion-Dollar Revenge

*Bound by the Italian's "I Do"*

### Scandalous Royal Weddings

*Crowning His Kidnapped Princess*
*Pregnant Innocent Behind the Veil*
*Rules of Their Royal Wedding Night*

Visit the Author Profile page
at Harlequin.com for more titles.

# *Michelle Smart*

---

# CHRISTMAS BABY WITH HER ULTRA-RICH BOSS

HARLEQUIN

PRESENTS

HARLEQUIN®
PRESENTS™

Recycling programs
for this product may
not exist in your area.

ISBN-13: 978-1-335-59294-1

Christmas Baby with Her Ultra-Rich Boss

Copyright © 2023 by Michelle Smart

For questions and comments about the quality of this book, please contact us at CustomerService@Harlequin.com.

Harlequin Enterprises ULC
22 Adelaide St. West, 41st Floor
Toronto, Ontario M5H 4E3, Canada
www.Harlequin.com

**Printed in U.S.A.**

# CHRISTMAS BABY WITH HER ULTRA-RICH BOSS

# CHAPTER ONE

TWO HUNDRED AND ten kilometres north of the Arctic Circle, adjacent to the Torne River, the main lodge of the Siopis Ice Hotel was filled with chattering staff. The wooden lodge, which served as the reception and administrative offices, and the cosy chalets surrounding it, were open all year round for guests to enjoy the changing of the seasons, but it was when November arrived and the river froze enough for the craftsmen and women to get to work, that the magic really happened. In the four years Lena Weir had worked there, she'd never failed to be awed by the talent and creativity and sheer hard work that went into creating what was known as The Igloo out of nothing but blocks of ice and snow; never failed, either, to sigh wistfully when spring arrived and the magical creation melted back into the river from which it was formed.

Today though, spring felt a world away. It was nearly 2 p.m. It could be midnight. The sun had made its last brief appearance three days ago. Lena, along with the rest of the staff and their guests, had stood outside and basked under its weak rays for the full twenty-six minutes it had graced them. It wouldn't show its face again other than as a brief glimmer on the horizon for another three weeks.

The lack of sun had never bothered her during her previous winters here in Sweden. She enjoyed them, liked experiencing what her mother had lived through for the first twenty years of her life. She struggled far more in the summer months when the opposite happened and the stars rarely came out and the sun never slept.

In three days the first guests of the winter season would arrive. Those adventurous enough and rich enough would spend a night in The Igloo itself. The activity happening in the lodge was the final staff meeting before the official winter opening of The Igloo. Welcoming the first guests through its doors was always a thrill. The exterior of the design was always the same, basically a giant igloo, but the interior was always different. The only constant was the sparkle of the ice, translucent through the carefully woven lights.

As the staff layered themselves for the biting outdoors, the reception phone rang. Sven being the closest picked it up, and in perfect English said, 'Siopis Ice Hotel, how can I help you?'

If he hadn't immediately looked at her, Lena would have missed the flicker of panic that crossed Sven's face as he listened to the caller. He nodded vigorously and ended the call saying, 'Of course. I will get the housekeeping team on it immediately.'

'What's wrong?' Lena asked. Everything at the Ice Hotel ran so smoothly that it was rare to see any of the staff flustered. Had one of the cabins' coffee machines stopped working? A guest greeted with an unmade bed? It couldn't be anything more serious than that if the housekeeping team was being called into action.

Turned out it could be.

'That was Magda. The six-month inspection has been brought forward.'

She raised an eyebrow but was unperturbed. Lena had nothing to hide. She'd privately thought scheduling the inspection for three days before Christmas was bonkers timing. Bringing it forward made a heap of sense.

But Sven hadn't finished. 'Mr Siopis is coming himself to do it.'

Lena actually felt the blood drain from her head down to her toes in a whoosh.

Gripping hard to the reception desk, she forced air into her lungs and managed to croak, 'When?'

Konstantinos Siopis only ever made one visit a year to the Ice Hotel and that was in the summer. He wasn't due back for another seven months.

Unsurprised at her reaction—no doubt Sven thought it entirely reasonable—he said, 'He will be here in four hours.'

Fighting her body's determination to drop into a ball and rock back and forth, Lena tightened her grip on the reception desk and did her best to keep the panic from her voice. 'You are going to tell house-keeping to sort a cabin out for him?'

Sven nodded.

'Okay. I will arrange for the car to collect him from the airport.' Sending their guests favourite mode of transport—the huskies and sledges—to collect him was out of the question. 'Did Magda say how long he will be here for?'

'No.'

She wouldn't chide Sven for not asking. Magda was as terrifying a PA as it was possible for the owner of a luxury hotel chain and investor in cutting-edge technology to get. She was almost as terrifying as her boss. Who also happened to be Lena's boss, too, and the ultimate boss of every member of staff there.

He also happened to be father of the secret baby growing inside her.

Konstantinos looked out at the unpitying darkness. Some people got a thrill out of endless nights and relentless cold but he wasn't one of them. Sun-drenched islands like his birthplace Kos were his natural habitat. He never felt the need to escape to colder climates, and generally worked his annual diary so he would always be somewhere the sun beat down.

Where his pilot was currently preparing to land, almost as north of Sweden as it was possible to get, the only illumination came from a smattering of lit-up homes and research centres and small tourist areas. The sun wouldn't show itself for weeks.

The landing went smoothly but the biting cold hit him the moment the cabin crew opened the door. A short walk later and he was in the back of a heated car and shaking his hat off. He supposed he should be grateful it wasn't snowing. Konstantinos's dark olive skin did not appreciate wet ice landing directly on it. His legs didn't appreciate having to spend extra time walking through it. The rest of him didn't appreciate having to wear layers of unstylish clothing to protect him from it.

As a child he'd watched Christmas movies with picture-perfect white settings and envied the children in them and the fun they had making snowballs and snowmen and sledging. His first personal experience of snow was aged twenty-one when he'd taken Cassia to New York for a long weekend. It had taken him all of five minutes to despise it. By the time he'd returned to Kos, he'd vowed to avoid the cold and snow for the rest of his life.

So why had he made the impulsive decision to delay his scheduled trip to Australia and instead head to a part of the world that currently provided none of the comforts he thought essential, namely sunshine?

It was standard practice in his organisation for each of his hospitality businesses to be inspected twice a year. Konstantinos's aversion to the cold meant he entrusted all his cold-climate northern hemisphere winter inspections to his specialist team. Early that morning he'd been woken by a call informing him that Nicos, director of said inspection team, had been admitted to hospital with gallstones and was likely to be off work for six weeks. Nicos was scheduled to inspect the Ice Hotel three days before Christmas, less than a month away.

The Siopis Ice Hotel was the jewel in Konstantinos's crown, a hotel complex that never failed to deliver year-round rave reviews. Each winter people from around the world flocked to stay the night in The Igloo, a magnificent structure built anew each autumn from ice and snow. Since its opening eight years ago, Konstantinos had deliberately timed his annual visits to the summer months when The Igloo had long melted in the spring thaw, and the permanent year-round log cabins were visited by wealthy adventurers seeking wilderness tours and rafting experiences.

Nicos's being out of action and the rest of the inspection team's schedules being full meant the Ice Hotel's inspection would have to be delayed. This wouldn't be a significant issue if Konstantinos hadn't five months earlier entrusted the running of it to Lena Weir, the youngest and least qualified candidate to apply for the general manager's role. Lena's weekly reports were as succinct and thorough as he'd come to expect from the individual managers of his hotels, the reviews as glowing as he'd come to expect, too, but only a thorough inspection could determine if things were as shiny internally as were projected externally. He would have to suck up his loathing of the cold and dark, and make the inspection himself. Thinking quickly, he'd determined that as it was his turn to spend Christmas with his family in Kos, the timings of the scheduled inspection would be cutting things too fine, especially if unexpected issues were revealed, so had made the decision to undertake the inspection immediately.

It was an impulsive decision he'd regretted as soon as he'd made it.

He'd never visited one of his businesses with such a tightness in his chest before, and for that he blamed himself and his stupidity of five months ago.

Since striking out on his own, Konstantinos had conducted a version of what his own father had done whenever hiring a new member of staff for the family restaurant, namely sharing a meal with the new recruit, the simple breaking of bread a gesture of welcome. As Konstantinos now hired thousands of people around the world, it had long been unfeasible for him to continue it, but the tradition held in its own way, those responsible for hiring anywhere within his organisation expected to take new staff members out for a meal, the expenses taken care of by the Siopis Group. As the most senior appointments were made by Konstantinos himself, he continued the tradition with staff appointed directly by him. Which was how he'd ended up sharing a meal with Lena Weir after promoting her to manager of his Ice Hotel.

Although the location was as remote as remote could be, there were a range of high-class eateries dotted around the site, including the hotel's very own Michelin-starred restaurant, which is where they'd dined. They'd made their way through the whole tasting menu, pairing each course with the recommended wine, and somehow managed to get through three bottles between them. It had seemed like the most natural thing in the world to walk her to her cabin, even more natural to accept her invitation of a coffee.

They'd been exceedingly polite to each other the next morning and he'd left Sweden reasonably certain it wouldn't affect their working relationship. He'd been given no reason to think otherwise since.

Lena Weir was no fool. She was a woman who did her homework—her tenacity in all things was one of the reasons he'd entrusted the job to her—and she would know a man didn't reach the age of thirty-seven without settling down or having any notable relationships unless that was exactly how he wanted it.

Shapes emerged through the car's headlights. They'd almost reached the hotel complex.

His chest tightened into a pin.

Konstantinos had never gotten drunk with an employee before. He'd certainly never slept with one.

It had been a mistake. They'd both agreed that the next morning.

It had been a mistake that would never be spoken of or alluded to again.

When the huge all-terrain car pulled up at the front of the all-year reception lodge, Lena avoided Sven's attempt to meet her gaze. She knew the fear she'd find in his stare would only feed the rancid panic gnawing in her stomach.

But her panic was not the same as Sven's or the other staff who, when told the owner was making a surprise visit, had started racing around like headless chickens. It was their reaction that had pulled her together, even if only superficially, and she'd clapped her hands together to get their attention.

'We all do our jobs to the high standard he expects of us so what is there to worry about?' she'd said, before pausing and adding with a half smile, 'Although, if anyone feels they might have cut some corners in some way, now would be a good time to rectify it.' A few members of staff had sheepishly scuttled out.

Lena knew whatever corners those staff had cut, they had been minor. Her staff worked hard, for their guests and each other. They were a solid team and had each other's backs. Konstantinos Siopis would not find anything here that did not meet his exacting standards. At least, she prayed he didn't. He paid his staff extremely well and was generous with the benefits written into their contracts, but in exchange he demanded perfection. A bad review demanded a thorough investigation, and any staff found to have been negligent in their duties could consider themselves lucky to get away with a written warning for a first offence. There were no second chances. In the five months Lena had been manager she'd only had to deal with three incidents of neglectful staff. Luckily, those minor infringements hadn't made it onto any review sites and she'd failed to put those infringements in writing on the staff's individual records. But there was no way Konstantinos could know this…could he? That would be grounds for him to dismiss her.

She swallowed the bile rising up her throat and watched Konstantinos unfold his long, rangy frame out of the back of the car. An abundance of strategically placed LED lights gave enough illumination for anyone to find their way around safely outside, the glow reminding her of the fairy lights her father used to drape around their garden at Christmas when she was a child.

Wrapped in a long lambswool coat that, even with the collar turned up, would give little protection against the cold, he trod his way over the compacted white snow towards the lodge door. Each step closer made the beat of Lena's heart heavier, and she had to stop her hands moving to protect her belly. Apart from the hotel's on-site doctor who was bound to confidentiality, no one knew she was pregnant. It was a secret she hugged fearfully to herself, a maternal instinct that had unfurled when the test had proved positive.

Lena could not afford to lose her job. Without it, she had no way to provide for her baby. Nowhere to live outside this remote corner of the world. Her parents' home in England would always be open to her but there was no room for her and a baby there, not with her tiny childhood bedroom now a makeshift pharmacy and medical equipment storage room for her sister. She had no savings other than what she'd squirrelled away since the pregnancy test had come up positive. Whatever savings her parents had amassed had been quickly depleted after the terrible accident Lena had walked away unscathed from but which had left Heidi needing twenty-four-hour care.

The man she should have been able to turn to, the father of her child, was almost at the door. Her weighty heart almost became stuck in her throat.

While Sven darted forward to open the door for him, Lena grabbed the thick folder she'd prepared and placed it in front of her belly, then sent a silent prayer that Konstantinos didn't pay too close attention to her figure. The heating inside the lodge was so good that most of the staff usually just wore their uniform polo shirts but in the past couple of weeks, Lena had taken to wearing the smart thick black sweater dress with an inbuilt collar the female customer-facing staff was provided with. Only the most eagle-eyed person would notice that beneath it were signs of a neat but developing bump. To play safe, she'd helped herself to an oversized sweater dress, which so far had been a successful means of disguising it.

Konstantinos stamped the snow stuck to the soles of his boots off at the mat before the door and stepped inside.

His gaze fixed straight onto the woman he'd spent the night with the last time he'd been here. Her large, dark brown eyes met his. A beat passed between them before a welcoming smile lit her face and she strode over to him, a folder clasped in one hand over her stomach, the other outstretched.

'Mr Siopis, this is an unexpected pleasure.'

'I'm sure,' he replied sardonically, clasping his fingers around hers in a businesslike fashion. A flash of warmth darted over and through his skin, and his hold on her tightened reflexively. Immediately, he released the hold and also released his stare to cast his gaze around the immaculate reception room, taking in the traditionally Swedish Christmas decorations and beautifully decorated fir adorning it. The scents of tinsel, cinnamon and orange permeated the air.

Even though the whole non-ice sections and cabins of the Ice Hotel were heated by geothermal means, the main lodge reception had an open log fire roaring, a welcome feature to the freezing cold guests on their arrival. He stepped over and placed his hands before it.

After a moment to gather himself, he turned his face back to Lena. He detected an apprehension that could almost be confused with fear. Both emotions were understandable. He, too, had felt an apprehension at seeing her again. At least, he thought it had been apprehension that had tied his stomach in knots and made his chest feel tight from the moment he'd made his decision to come here. A committed short-term monogamist since Theo and Cassia's betrayal, Konstantinos had never been a man for one-night stands. The few he'd enjoyed had been hookups with strangers, women he never expected to see again. Women he'd never had to see again. Women he'd never wanted to see again. None of them had lingered in his memories.

Lena had. Lingered, that is. Another reason why breaching professional boundaries was a bad idea. Konstantinos owned twenty-three hotels and invested in numerous other businesses. Since their night together, his heart had skipped a beat that was both unprofessional and inexplicable whenever her name pinged into his inbox. Her emails, always concise and professional, were the only emails he found himself reading twice. Her weekly reports were the only reports he read with more than a scan for the pertinent information.

Never again, he told himself grimly, again. Mixing business with pleasure was a recipe for disaster he'd learned the hard way. To have lapsed as he had, even with the excuse of alcohol thrown into the mix, was a mistake he was forced to regret every time Lena's name diverted his attention from whatever work he had in hand. And now she stood before him in the flesh, her dark brown hair with the glimmer of russet tones loose around her shoulders, one side tucked behind a small pixie-like ear, framing an oval face that any man would look twice at. Large, velvet brown eyes. Pretty, straight nose. Wide, generous lips. All atop a slender frame with breasts far more generous than the clothes she wore would…

He cut his thoughts off. He should not still be able to feel the weight of Lena's breasts on the palm of his hand.

'Has a cabin been made ready for me?' he asked

curtly. Here, in the middle of nowhere, there was a rule that a cabin should always be kept free in case of emergency.

'It has,' she confirmed. 'I have the accounts for the last quarter ready if—'

'The business side will be dealt with later,' he interrupted. 'My first priority is to tour The Igloo.' Get that part over with and then he could spend the rest of his short stay here out of the damned cold.

She nodded and gave another of her bright smiles and indicated the tall Scandinavian manning the reception desk with a young Spanish woman. 'Perhaps Sven can—'

'No. You're the manager. It is for you to show me around it.'

Her lips twitched and another flash of apprehension flickered in her eyes but Lena's smile didn't waver. 'Of course. I only suggested Sven because his father was the lead architect and Sven was involved in creating one of the art rooms.'

'Do you not have the same knowledge of its creation?' he challenged.

'I do, as do all the staff.'

'Good. Sven can show me to my cabin. Meet me back here in thirty minutes and we can get started.'

'Do you want to walk or ski to The Igloo? Or go by snowmobile?' Lena's preferred way of getting around the complex was with skis. It didn't actually involve any real skiing in the hurling down a mountain sense; it was just an easier way of getting around in these conditions than walking.

'We will walk,' he answered, without any hesitation.

'As you wish.'

He met her eyes, gave a sharp nod, and set off through the reception room with Sven in tow to the back of the lodge and to the most direct route to the cabins.

As soon as the door closed behind him, Lena expelled a long breath and closed her eyes.

Well, that had to rank in the top two most excruciating moments of her life. She couldn't decide if it trumped the morning after the night before.

She'd gazed at Konstantinos sleeping in her bed with her heart thumping wildly, then climbed out, sniffed his discarded shirt as she'd put it on, and thrown open the blackout curtains. The bright summer sun had kissed skin still marked with the passion of Konstantinos's mouth, and she had whipped around to face him, joyous laughter bubbling up her throat, legs already preparing to spring back to the bed and wake him with a kiss when she'd found his eyes open. The expression in them had made the laughter die in her throat.

'Last night was a mistake.'

Those five words had pierced her. In less time than it took to blink, the joy she'd been full to the brim with had seeped out of the hole his piercing words had made.

She'd hugged his shirt tighter around herself and nodded. 'Yes.'

He'd thrown the sheets off and climbed off the

bed. 'It is not a habit of mine to sleep with the staff. Rest assured it will not happen again.'

Pride made her say, 'Let's just put it down to too much wine and forget about it.'

Green eyes more piercing than his tongue fixed on her again. 'You can do that?'

'I'm an adult and quite capable of separating my personal life from my professional one. Last night was a slip made when I was off duty and one I doubt either of us would have made if we'd been sober. How about we both chalk it down to experience and never speak of it again?'

She'd forced herself to take the weight of his stare as he sized her up, judging the value of her words. Eventually, he'd given a short nod. 'As long as we are both of the same mind.'

'Totally.' She'd mimed zipping her lips.

He'd almost smiled.

# CHAPTER TWO

ONCE LENA HAD added a few extra layers over her work clothes, she carried her all-in-one snowsuit from the storeroom to the reception to wait for Konstantinos, only to find he was already there, back turned to her, grilling Sven.

Her heart quivered and jumped painfully, and she closed her eyes and breathed deeply through her nose, just for a moment, just long enough to catch her emotions before they spilled over.

She hadn't expected that seeing Konstantinos in the flesh again would feel so emotional. Pregnancy hormones, she supposed, although it pained her to suspect that she would still be reacting in the same way if she hadn't conceived.

Lena hadn't expected to fall into bed with him. Until he'd walked her back to her cabin and her heart had suddenly lurched to know their evening together was over, she hadn't considered him the slightest bit attractive. The uncharitable would go so far as to call Konstantinos Siopis ugly, what with his angular features, his long, sharp, prominent nose that bent at an angle, bowed lips always fixed in a straight line, and deep-set eyes ringed in dark shadows and topped with bushy black eyebrows. He wore his thick, curly hair cropped short and clad his long, rangy figure in varying shades of black. That he rarely smiled only enhanced the impression of brooding, almost vampiric unattractive menace. That his fang teeth were a teensy bit longer than the rest only added to this. If he were an actor, he'd be typecast as the baddie, every time.

But he'd smiled that evening *and* without his face cracking. His eyes—a gorgeous clear green she'd not even noticed until sitting opposite him in the restaurant—had lost their coldness and, if not softened, warmed. Possibly it had been the wine goggles she'd ended up wearing but the longer their meal went on, the more fascinating she'd found his face and the deep olive of his skin, which always looked in need of a shave, and the more fascinating she'd found the deep, gravelly voice she'd always thought faintly terrifying. Konstantinos's English was so precise and his Greek accent so heavy that to her ears he'd always sounded as if he was barely concealing impatience. That evening his tone, like his eyes, had warmed. By the time they'd reached her cabin her whole body thrummed, hot, dizzying awareness rocketing through.

It hurt to look at him now. It hurt to hear his voice.

Her body had come alive for him. It had sung to him. She'd gazed at his sleeping face the next morning with a heart clambering to break free and then climbed out of her bed and practically bounced to the window like a spring lamb to throw the curtains open.

Inexplicably, it had been the single happiest moment of her life in six long years.

And then he'd woken and delivered those awful words that had punctured her inexplicable joy.

As she walked apprehensively in her three pairs of socks over the thick carpet to him, she wondered for the umpteenth time how she'd gone from finding Konstantinos completely unattractive to incredibly sexy in the space of one evening.

Noticing her approach, he gave a short nod of acknowledgement and continued his grilling of Sven, forcing Lena to stand around like a hovering lemon and do her best not to let her eyes keep falling on him. He'd removed the dark suit and long overcoat he'd arrived in, his lean frame now wrapped in black jeans and a thick black sweater. She hoped he had thermal layers on beneath it. Layers were the key to survival here. Multiple layers. She wouldn't ask him, though. Konstantinos was not a man who encouraged unsolicited advice.

She wished she didn't care if he'd layered up. She doubted he cared if she had. She doubted he'd given her a second thought since he'd left her cabin five months ago.

'You're ready?' he asked a short while later, finally fixing his attention on her.

'I just need to put my snowsuit and boots on.'

He nodded and strode to one of the armchairs by

the open fire where a black thermal snowsuit had been draped over it. Snatching it up, he sat down to put his feet into the legs and then stood back up to pull it to his waist, past calves and thighs far more muscular than would be believed when clothed.

From the other side of the room, Lena did the same with her too-large staff-issue blue-and-white thermal suit, trying not to watch him, trying not to let her mind remember the strength in his arms as he slid them into his suit's sleeves, or think about the defined muscularity of his abdomen and chest, or the thick black hair that covered it as he zipped it up to his chin. When he sat back down and forced his huge feet into the all-weather boots that would allow him to tread on the ice without danger of slipping, a sliver of fear crawled up her spine.

Lena had toured the latest incarnation of The Igloo just three days ago. Her own boots were as sturdy and ice resistant as Konstantinos's, but she'd had a real terror of losing her footing and landing on her backside. It wasn't fear of hurting her bottom that had frightened her but fear of hurting her baby. She knew there was little danger of slipping in the Ice Hotel, but knowing something intellectually was a lot different than feeling it emotionally. Today she had the added danger of touring it with her baby's father, the one person she so desperately needed to keep her pregnancy secret from. Konstantinos's discovering she was pregnant was the single biggest danger to her baby. She couldn't risk him finding out yet. She just couldn't. She hadn't saved enough money yet to support herself for longer than a fortnight and had none of the supplies a newborn baby needed.

She hated that she had to keep it from him, but the coldness emanating in waves from him was unnerving enough to convince her that she'd made the right decision. There was little chance of him accepting the baby as his without a paternity test and every chance he would sack her on the spot.

Both fully suited and booted, thick hats rammed on their heads and thick scarves wound around their necks and half their faces—Lena always felt claustrophobic with a balaclava on and only wore one in blizzards—they lifted their hoods over their heads and stepped out into the bracing cold.

The vast complex that constituted the Siopis Ice Hotel was dominated by two main sections. One was the year-round area centred by the main lodge reception. Dotted around it were the guest log cabins, restaurants, boutiques, spa, the buildings that housed the snowmobiles and ski hire, and all the other facilities that enabled them to cater to their guests' every adventurous or more sedate desires. To its left was the path that led to the second section, commonly known as The Igloo.

A ten-minute walk from the all-year reception, the path to The Igloo was lit by the same magical quality lights used to guide guests and staff to the lodge and cabins. The only sounds as they made their way to it were the low throb of music from one of the occupied cabins and their own breaths, each exhale accompanied by a white cloud of expelled air.

'How long are you planning to stay here?' Lena asked as they passed the ice rink and snow-covered permanent cabin used as The Igloo's reception and the huge, cleverly lit dome of The Igloo itself emerged fully from the darkness, and she could bear the tension tautening her every sinew no more.

'One night,' he said with a clipped tone of voice that suggested it was more than enough time.

'One night too long?' she queried wryly while inwardly heaving a giant sigh of relief. That meant he expected the inspection to be wrapped up by the end of day tomorrow.

One night was manageable. With any luck, he'd leave Sweden none the wiser about the child growing in her belly.

When she did tell him, he would be furious. The green eyes that had flared with such hunger would fill with loathing; the mouth that had kissed her so passionately would curve in disgust. There would not be an ounce of warmth in his voice.

She wished she could blame him but she couldn't.

'At this time of year, one hour is too long to spend here.'

'Not a fan of the cold?'

'No,' he answered shortly.

The entry to The Igloo was a permanent structure. The sensor doors slid quickly open and they entered a world of sparkling white. Before them lay the welcome room adorned with long chairs and low tables made entirely of clear ice, and with a fireplace carved into the wall that gave the illusion of white flames flickering in it. It was a sight replicated year after year that never failed to bring a gasp of awe to their guests' mouths. It was an awe that only increased when they were led through the rest of it.

The cold of the Ice Hotel's interior sucked the air from Konstantinos's lungs. He knew it was warmer inside—if you could call minus five degrees warm—than outside but being plunged into an ice-white surround played tricks on the mind. The immediate plunge into silence didn't help with the mind tricks. He tightened his hood and kept his gaze on the giant dome he'd stepped into rather than the woman he'd entered it with.

He was in half a mind to leave when the tour of this icebox was done with. He could fly to his hotel in the south of Spain where the weather was currently balmy, stay there for the night, and then fly as planned to Australia to deal with his many southern hemisphere business interests until Christmas. Have Nicos complete the full inspection when he was back to full health.

To leave Sweden immediately, though, would be a sign of defeat, not just of the cold but of Lena. He would not be pushed out of his own hotel because of the tightness that pulled sharply at his stomach every time he looked at her. She was a beautiful woman. That was a fact he'd registered on a superficial level at their first meeting much in the same way he noted the colour of a person's clothing. Until that damned celebratory dinner, she was just another employee. Just another face. Another name.

That was all she was to him now, he reminded himself firmly. Just another employee. These strange feelings currently gripping him and making his insides feel hot and cold at the same time were solely because this was a novel situation he found himself in. A situation he wouldn't be in if he hadn't been so damned stupid as to sleep with her.

Clenching his teeth, he inhaled the frigid air into his tight lungs and forced his attention back to where it should be. On the jewel of his crown, the giant Igloo.

Off the vast main dome were the warrens of iced tunnels that led to the dozens of individual rooms, and they set off into the nearest one. The tunnels were higher than he remembered, the walls thicker.

The rooms they toured were each individually crafted and therefore unique, the majority containing nothing but a large bed made of ice and topped with a thick mattress that itself was topped with reindeer hide.

'Have you spent a night here?' he asked when they went down yet more ice steps and into a room carved into a forest scene with pine trees and reindeers, the bed having the effect of rising off the forest floor. The customer-facing staff was encouraged to sleep in the hotel during the window between completion—not that it was ever completed. Ongoing maintenance was needed for such a huge, complex structure—and the first guests' arrival, but this was not mandatory.

'Once. My first winter here.'

'And?'

'I found it too claustrophobic to want to do it again.'

Surprised, he gazed up at the high forest scene above his head then back at her with an expression that demanded explanation.

She shook her head. 'When the lights are turned off…'

'Explain,' he commanded.

'It's the darkness,' she said with a shrug.

'It is always dark this time of year.' As dark as it was cold.

'Not like it is in here. It's a completely different experience. In here, the walls are so thick that nothing penetrates it, no light or sound…you must hear it now, the absolute silence. And I stayed in a room with a door.' Most of the ice rooms had fur curtains for doors, which let slivers of light in from the tunnel corridor LEDs that were kept on at all times for safety reasons, but a handful had real doors designed to cope with subzero temperatures. Those rooms were the largest and most spectacular of them all and guests paid a premium for them. Lena had hardly believed her luck when she'd been appointed one for the night. That was until the door closed, her room's lights went off, and she'd been pitched into absolute blackness.

'Outside there is always some form of light, whether from the moon and the stars or, if you're *really* lucky, from the aurora borealis, but in here…' She rubbed her arms and shivered. 'It's like sleeping in a tomb.'

'Be sure not to tell our guests that,' he said sharply.

'Of course I won't,' she said, stung at his tone. The vast majority of their guests loved the experience. 'But you asked me to explain and I explained because that's how it felt to me at the time, and it does say on all our literature and online information that staying in The Igloo isn't suitable for claustrophobic guests. Those who suffer from it stay in the cabins.'

'So why did you stay in it if you suffer from claustrophobia?'

'I didn't know I did until that night.' Not until she'd been lying in the pitch-black and found herself thrown back to that terrible night when she'd been trapped in the dark with her sister, praying for Heidi to wake up, praying for help to come quickly. She'd imagined she could still smell her sister's blood.

He contemplated her for another moment then indicated the fur-lined ice door. 'I have seen enough of the rooms. Take me to the bar.'

The bar was to the back of The Igloo, close to the ice tunnel that took their guests to the permanent non-ice heated changing rooms, and reached by climbing a number of wide steps. Lena sat on a fur-lined ice booth and kept quiet while Konstantinos took it all in. She had the distinct feeling her confession of claustrophobia had irritated him. No doubt he wasn't scared of anything at all.

In her opinion, the creator of the bar had surpassed himself this year. The craftsmanship and artistry were incredible. It was like being in a swish wine bar with wooden panelling and optics and pumps, except one made entirely of ice. Witty pictures hung on the walls; each table had beer mats carved into them…there was even a coat stand with coats hanging on it. All carved from ice. The only things in the bar that weren't illusions were the fur lining on the chairs to prevent frostbite and the drinks they served. While Lena would never wish to spend another night in The Igloo, that didn't stop her revelling in the sheer spectacle of it.

She watched Konstantinos examine a shot glass made of ice, real fascination in his expression.

'Drink?' he surprised her by asking.

She shook her head.

The semi-frozen vodka poured thickly and when the ice glass was filled, he drank the shot in one go. He gave an exaggerated blink as it slid down his throat then screwed the lid back on the bottle. 'Too cold for my tastes. Let's return to the lodge.'

Konstantinos's arrogant assumption that he'd be able to conduct the tour with his business head on had proven a fallacy he rued darkly once they were back on the path to the main lodge. The longer they'd spent in The Igloo, the greater his awareness had grown that by his side was the woman who'd lingered in his head when she should have evaporated from it, and the greater his resentment. Whether his resentment was aimed at Lena or himself or both of them, he couldn't say. He'd disliked watching her tentative movements in The Igloo and the way she'd touched the walls with every step she took, her movements much as if the ice beneath her feet scared her, which it couldn't, not with her being a seasoned pro on it.

Disliked it because there had been a vulnerability to her movements, which had disturbed him to even notice, but not half as disturbing as the compulsion to offer his hand for support, which in itself wasn't half as disturbing as the extra ice that had slivered in his veins when she'd described her claustrophobia, and an image of Lena herself entombed had flashed in his mind.

He should have opted to take the snowmobiles. If he had, they'd be back at the lodge by now and the crowding memories of the night they'd spent together would already be dimming amidst the noise of other people.

'How are you finding your role here?' he asked abruptly. The way he was currently feeling, the idea of shutting himself away with Lena in her office was intolerable. Get the questions he wanted answered by her done now and over with, spend the night going through the books—alone—and then get out of this place.

'Good, thanks.'

'What about the workload? You find it manageable?' He should not be hoping she would confess to finding it too hard and resign on the spot.

'It's nothing I didn't expect when I applied for the role,' she answered.

'And the responsibility? It is a big step going from duty manager to general manager.' It was a responsibility not everyone was cut out for. Hopefully, she would admit to being one of those people.

'It is,' she agreed, 'but I have a great team around me. Everyone pulls their weight.'

'Anything you have concerns about or feel needs my attention?'

'Nothing that's occurred since my last weekly report.'

They'd reached the lodge. Stopping to stamp the snow stuck to their boots, he asked, 'You haven't held anything back from me?'

If he hadn't glanced at her he would have missed the flicker in her eyes.

She gave a quick shake of her head and said equally quickly, 'I report everything that needs reporting.'

Narrowing his eyes, Konstantinos wondered if the colour in her cheeks was purely a side effect of the cold, or down to her having just told a blatant lie. He was well aware his managers sanitised their reports for his reading, failing to include minor incidents that he should, by rights and by contract, be kept apprised of. He let them go. He couldn't micromanage every aspect—that was what he paid the managers to do for him and he had to trust their judgement on what was deemed serious enough to notify him about. Occasionally though, he would learn of incidents that had no place being swept under the carpet. The question was whether Lena was covering up for something minor or something more serious. Her reaction made him suspect the latter.

They stepped inside. Konstantinos pulled his hat off, unzipped his snowsuit, and appraised her flushed face one last time. 'I believe your shift has finished. Leave your office unlocked for me. There are members of staff I wish to speak to.'

She'd made no attempt to remove any of her own clothing, and now he detected a noticeable flicker of fear in her dark brown eyes. 'About me?'

By now convinced she was hiding or covering up something, he smiled tightly. 'Everything appears to be in order but I take nothing at face value. I will call you in if I discover anything that needs your attention or explaining. Enjoy your personal time.'

Long past midnight, stripping off in the privacy of a log cabin far more luxurious than the last cabin he'd slept in whilst there, Konstantinos was unsure if he was relieved or disappointed that the only misdemeanours Lena had failed to notify him of were so minor it would have annoyed him if she'd added them to a report. He'd been disgruntled to find that all the reasons he'd promoted her a good few years sooner than he would anyone else in her position had proven sound and that Lena was an exemplary manager. She had the respect and loyalty of her whole staff and, in some cases, adoration.

Glass of Scotch in hand, he climbed into the rolltop bath he'd run to warm his frozen bones, sank under the hot water, and tried not to mentally plot the route to Lena's cabin. She would have upgraded since their night together, staff accommodation being consummate to position. Only staff with a managerial title had a cabin to themselves. The general manager was granted the largest of them all.

After a large sip, he leaned his head back, closed his eyes, and tried to breathe out the tightness in his chest and the heavy ache in his loins.

He should have taken that woman in California up on her offer the other week. He'd attended a tech investment conference—Konstantinos's businesses were varied—and her interest in him had been obvious from the moment she'd read his name tag. It never ceased to amaze him how his sex appeal grew once his name was recognised. Beautiful women who barely gave him a second glance when he was anonymous suddenly switched into beguiling flirt mode. A cynic would think it was his money they were after. A cynic, if in the mood, would take them up on their unspoken offers and enjoy a night of no-strings sex. If he'd accepted the Californian woman's offer of a nightcap in her room, an offer made as she fingered the length of his tie, he could have purged himself. Five months of celibacy wasn't healthy. He'd never gone this long between lovers before, which only brought his thoughts back to Lena, the last woman he'd been with.

Konstantinos threw the rest of his Scotch down his throat and swallowed it in one gulp.

Come the morning and he wouldn't hang around. He'd keep appearances up, congratulate Lena on running a tight ship, and then get the hell out of this god-forsaken place until the summer.

# CHAPTER THREE

LENA DABBED CONCEALER under her eyes to hide the dark circles that had formed after her terrible night's lack of sleep. Many more nights like that and her circles would be as dark as Konstantinos's.

A smear of balm over her lips and then she donned her snowsuit over her work clothes and set off on the short journey to the lodge. Apprehension and fear had compressed into knots in her stomach. She'd spent the whole night on tenterhooks waiting for her phone to ring and for Konstantinos's unemotional, gravelly voice to invite her back to the lodge so he could sack her.

She'd been convinced she was going to lose her job, certain he'd discover the incident of the missing petty cash—whoever had taken it had replaced the money the next day—and the drunken scuffle between two members of staff that hadn't been witnessed by any of the guests but which had resulted in broken furniture in the staff lounge. That, too, had been resolved the very next morning with a brisk hungover handshake, a bear hug, and a lot of glue.

After hanging up her snowsuit and checking her small bump was still hidden beneath the oversized sweater, Lena headed to her office.

Konstantinos was already there, sat at her desk, unshaven but dressed in a shirt and tie and black sweater, looking at something on her computer. Her knotted stomach lurched and her heart made that same quivering jump from yesterday.

He must have turned the heating up. The air in her usually balmy office currently felt more like the air in the sauna.

Somehow, she managed to inject a form of brightness into her tone. 'Good morning. Is everything okay?'

He glanced up from the screen and gave a short nod. 'You have an email from one of the grocery suppliers. They will be late with their delivery today.'

'You're going through my emails?'

'Your work emails,' he corrected. 'And I wasn't going through them. The notification popped up on the screen two minutes ago. Would you have a problem with me looking at them?'

It was the narrowed scrutiny of his green eyes that made her cheeks burn, but she kept her frame and tone steady. 'Not at all. How's the inspection going?' If she was about to lose her job then get it over with. The wait for feedback had become more than she could endure.

'I'm done.'

'Already?'

He leaned back on the seat. *Her* seat. Those deep-set green eyes bore into her. 'I congratulate you. You delegate well. The place is spotless. The guests are happy. The staff are happy. You run a tight ship.'

Her relief was such that she blew out the air she'd been holding and laughed. 'Phew.'

'You sound surprised.'

She pulled at the ends of her hair, which she'd left loose. 'I was under no illusion that my perspective of how I run things might differ from your perspective.'

'If your perspective is that you run things to a high standard then we are in agreement.' He looked at his watch and rose to his feet. 'Time for me to leave.'

Instead of jubilation that he was leaving so soon, there was another, stronger lurch in her stomach, more like a plummet, and a definite tremor in her voice as she politely asked, 'Where are you heading to next?'

'Australia.'

'The climate more to your liking?'

His lips twitched before he grunted his agreement and thrust his hand across the desk to her.

The beats of her heart increasing in weight and tempo, she stretched her arm out. The instant his long, warm fingers wrapped around hers, all the organs in her body contracted then released with a burst.

'Until the summer,' he said briskly.

The compulsion to throw herself into his arms and confess that they were having a baby and beg him to stay and share her joy and be a father to it was so strong and so sudden she almost staggered under the weight of it.

His eyes crinkled with concern. 'Is something the matter?'

Releasing her hand from his, she swallowed and shook her head. 'Just a bit warm in here,' she whispered. It wasn't a lie. The room was sweltering.

And what wasn't a lie, either, was that she didn't want him to go. As terrifying as the whole situation was, as terrifying as Konstantinos's being here was, and the inherent danger that came with his discovering the pregnancy when he had so much power over her fate...in that moment the thought of him leaving was close to unbearable.

He stared at her a beat longer then gave one of his sharp nods and stepped around her desk.

Another beat later and he was gone from her office. All that remained were the remnants of his citrusy cologne.

Konstantinos's car hadn't left the complex when he realised he'd left his phone by the computer in Lena's office.

Telling his driver to give him two minutes, self-recrimination roiled in his guts. If he hadn't been so keen to get away from her he wouldn't have forgotten the damned thing and now he had to go back in there and see her one more time. With any luck, she'd have left the office to run an errand somewhere and he wouldn't have to look into those large brown eyes and be transported back to the night he'd lost himself in her.

All these months he'd done his best to forget. Time should have put enough distance to make it nothing but a vague memory, but seeing her again had made it all slam back into his consciousness and it was no longer just the weight of her breasts against the palms of his hands he could still feel, but the silkiness of Lena's skin compressed against his and the exquisite bliss of being buried so deeply inside her. When she'd walked into the office, his tongue had suddenly tingled to remember the taste of her, a deep jolt of heat in his loins to recall the scent that had lingered in the air after they had collapsed in each other's arms.

He could still see, vividly, the way her eyes had widened when he'd first entered her, hear the intake of breath that had turned into a moan that had fed his desire for her in a way that had blown away every sexual experience he'd ever had before her.

Was it any wonder he'd felt it so necessary to leave her office?

He would not linger. He would grab his phone and get the hell out and stay the hell out.

Nodding at Anya, one of the women working the reception desk, and at the bundled-up couple checking in, he strode to the office.

Lena was opening the window, her back to him. She'd removed her sweater to reveal a fitted plain white long-sleeved top that enhanced the silhouette of her trim figure over her tight-fit black trousers.

She'd put a little weight on since their night together, he observed dimly.

She turned her head and visibly jumped with shock to see him.

'I left my phone behind,' he explained tersely, grabbing his phone and shoving it into his back pocket.

She didn't say a word, just stared at him with a look that reminded him strongly of a deer trapped in the glare of headlights.

He left the office as quickly as he'd entered it. His hand was on the door that connected to the reception when his feet brought him to a halt.

Something, some sixth sense, was thumping for attention in the back of his brain. The thumping extended to the rest of him.

Mouth suddenly dry, he turned slowly and strode with leaden feet back to the office.

He pushed the door open.

Lena's arms were in the sleeves of her sweater and she was in the process of pulling it over her head. There was a frantic quality in her movements, and when she tugged it down over her protruding belly and spotted him standing there, she no longer looked like a trapped deer. She looked like a *guilty* trapped deer.

For the longest passage of time her terrified eyes remained glued to his.

Blood pumped hard through him. Getting air into his lungs became impossible.

'Lift your sweater,' he commanded hoarsely.

Her face crumpled and she folded her arms protectively beneath her breasts and over her stomach.

He breathed deeply and lifted his chin. 'Do not make me repeat myself again, Lena. Lift your sweater up.'

It was hearing Konstantinos say her name for the first time since he'd arrived back in Sweden that broke Lena. The iciness in his voice. Her nightmare was coming to life but in this one there was no way of waking herself before the worst happened.

The tears she'd been holding back all these months broke free and rolled down her cheeks. With shaking hands, she gripped the hem of her sweater and pulled it up over her pregnant belly.

While he stared without blinking at her stomach, her baby moved inside her. She didn't know if he saw the movement but the impassivity on his face changed and he staggered back and fell into the visitor chair, the colour leeching from his olive skin.

Hands gripping his knees, he bowed his head. His shoulders rose and fell in almost exaggerated movements before he slowly lifted his face back up to meet her eyes. 'Is it mine?'

She tried to nod but her body was shaking too hard and all she could manage was a whispered, 'Yes.'

His face contorted into a frightening mix of rage and comprehension and, fury etched in his every sinew, he shot back to his feet. 'You lying, deceitful, poisonous—'

Only by the skin of his teeth did Konstantinos stop himself from uttering the cruel curse he wanted to throw at her. White-hot, rabid fury had infected every part of him, an anger so strong that he turned on his heel and stormed out of the office lest the poison consuming him erupted.

Uncaring that the snow had started to fall, he flung the emergency exit door open and stamped out onto the treated path at the rear of the reception lodge. On either side of the path snow was piled as high as his knees, and he scooped a load into his hands, packed it into as tight a ball as he could manage, and hurled it through the air with a roar. And then scooped more snow.

By the time he'd worked the worst of his fury out of him, he was soaked to the skin, his lungs were burning, and his hands frozen. Making a real effort to control his breathing and the rage still boiling in his veins, he went back inside.

Lena, her eyes red and her face blotchy from crying, was sitting on the visitor chair with a tissue clutched in her hand.

'Get your snowsuit on and come with me,' he snarled.

'Come where?' she croaked.

'My cabin, where we can speak without being disturbed...' A thought penetrated the fury in his brain. 'I assume no one else has been given it yet?'

She shook her head.

He stuck his head out the door and tersely shouted, 'Anya, keep my cabin reserved for me until further notice and call Sven in—he's in charge until further notice, too.' Then he looked again at the deceitful face of the woman who'd deliberately kept that she'd conceived his child a secret from him. 'Snowsuit.'

Feeling as sick as she'd ever been in her life, Lena obeyed, scuttling out to the staff storeroom and hurriedly donning a snowsuit, hat, scarf, and boots.

'Are you not going to change, too?' she tentatively asked when she returned to the office.

'What's the point?' he said bitterly. 'I'm already halfway to frostbite.'

The look on his face told her not to bother arguing with him.

They left through the same rear door Konstantinos had used to work his fury into the snow. The usually pristine mound of snow lining the path had had gouges taken out of it from where he'd made his furious snowballs. She'd watched with her hand over her mouth from the window, her heart aching and her head reeling at his raging anguish.

She welcomed the cold air she breathed in through the falling snow and by the time they reached his cabin, her mind felt clearer and sharper. She wished the rest of her felt clearer, too, but guilt and apprehension lay too heavily inside her for that. But there was a smidgen of relief mingled in her churning emotions. Konstantinos knew.

His learning of the pregnancy was the only thing she no longer had to fear. The rest of her worries and nightmares could still come to pass.

Inside the luxury cabin that was at least ten times

the size of her own, Lena stripped down to her work uniform while Konstantinos hung up his sodden coat in the heated cupboard by the entry door, and removed his soaked shoes and socks. Her heart twisted to see the snowflakes glistening on his black hair. Despite the warmth of the cabin, he must be freezing.

'You should have a bath to get warm,' she said quietly.

'Do not feign concern for my well-being,' he snapped, then yanked his sweater off, ripped his tie from around his neck, undid the top three buttons of his shirt, and whipped that off, too. The wet clothes all landed like puddles on the floor.

The last Lena saw of him was his ramrod straight back as he stormed into the bathroom and slammed the door shut behind him. A short moment later came the sound of running water.

Needing to keep herself occupied for fear of driving herself crazy with her fearful thoughts, she gathered Konstantinos's discarded clothes, intending to place them in the laundry box situated by the main door to stop sodden clothes from damaging the wooden flooring. For reasons she couldn't begin to comprehend, she pressed her nose into the bundle. The scent of his cologne made fresh tears swim in her eyes and, feeling choked and sicker than ever, she dropped the bundle into the box.

Each cabin came equipped with its own drinks station. Knowing Konstantinos took his coffee black, she slotted an espresso pod into the machine then made herself a hot chocolate. Once both drinks were done, she hesitated before helping herself to a miniature Scotch from the mini-bar and pouring it into his coffee. She knew she could have done with a stiff drink herself when she'd first discovered she really was pregnant.

At the bathroom door, she hesitated again before gently knocking on it. 'I've made you a hot drink,' she called, and wished she didn't sound so tremulous.

The door swung open. A cloud of warm, citrusy steam escaped.

Konstantinos, phone in hand, wearing only a towel around his snake hips, glowered down at her.

At five foot five, Lena wasn't particularly short but in that moment she felt tiny. Almost a foot taller than her, it was only when Konstantinos was undressed that his full strength and muscularity became apparent. Clothed, his masculinity was almost threatening in its intensity. She'd never known anyone so rampantly *male*. Undressed, there was a raw, rugged beauty to his physique that had stolen her breath the first time she'd seen him naked and now brought her close to spilling hot coffee over herself.

His gaze dropped accusingly to her hand.

She swallowed the moisture that had filled her throat and mouth and whispered, 'It'll help warm you.'

A pulse throbbed on his jaw. His chest rose and then, fingers brushing against hers, took the cup from her hand, gave a sound that could be interpreted as grudging gratitude, and closed the door.

Lena blew air out of her mouth and pressed a

hand to her chest, the other to her swelling bump. She would take it as a positive sign that he'd accepted the drink.

Miserably, she sat on one of the armchairs and thought back to a time when looking for the tiniest positive sign was all that had kept her sane. The blinks that showed Heidi understood what was being said to her. The first smile. The first attempt at speaking. The first successful attempt at speaking. And then the knowledge had come that this was as good as it was going to get, that her sister had reached the limit in her recovery. There would be no more new positives.

How could Heidi not have resented Lena for her health, resented that Lena had walked away physically whole while Heidi was condemned to a life of paralysis? It made her want to weep to think of the life Heidi should be leading. She *had* wept. Oceans of tears. But those tears didn't change anything. Heidi would never be a mother and have the family of her own she'd craved since they were little girls. Lena hadn't given two thoughts to having children until she'd missed her period. She was only twenty-five. Children and family had been years away…until they weren't.

Feeling more movement in her belly, she closed her eyes and rubbed it, wondering again how Heidi would take the news she was going to be an aunt when Lena told her family on her leave next month. She imagined the shocked but delighted smile but—

The bathroom door opened.

Lena's eyes snapped open and her thoughts scuttled away.

Dressed only in a complementary grey Siopis robe that was too short for his tall frame and yet still managed to look as if it had been designed with Konstantinos in mind, he carried his cup to the coffee machine and slid another pod into it. 'Can I get you anything?'

The offer brought a lump to her throat. 'No, thank you.'

As she'd done, he poured a miniature Scotch into his coffee then carried it to the armchair beside hers, straightened his robe, and sat down.

Although outwardly calmer, she could feel the tension vibrating through his frame, sensed he was holding on to his anger by a whisker, and when he finally fixed his green eyes on her, the coldness in them made her quail.

'How certain are you the child is mine?'

'Completely certain.'

His top lip curved. 'Be very careful, Lena. I am aware of the amount of bed hopping that takes place amongst the staff here. Are you positive no other man could be the father?'

'One hundred per cent positive. You're the only man I've been with in six years.'

Something dark sparked in his eyes. The pulse in his clenched jaw set off again. 'You expect me to believe I am the only man you have been intimate with in six years?'

'It's the truth.'

His cold gaze didn't leave hers. He was weighing her up, she realised. Judging whether or not to believe her.

All she could do was stare back and hope he recognised the truth in her eyes. If he chose not to believe her…

Her whole body trembled. She knew what the consequences would be if he decided her claims of his paternity were a lie. Destitution until the baby was born and she could force a paternity test.

Still staring intently at her, he took a long drink of his coffee before placing the china cup on the small round table to the side of his chair. 'If you are telling the truth then answer me this,' he said in a low growl. 'If I am the father of your child what in hell gave you the right to hide it from me?'

# CHAPTER FOUR

THE STRICKEN EXPRESSION on Lena's face made no impression on Konstantinos. If anything, it disgusted him. He'd done the maths. She had to be five months pregnant. She must have known for four of those months; three months if he was being generous. At least three months in which she'd kept the secret of the life they'd supposedly conceived together from him.

To expect him to believe he was the only man she'd been with in six years when she'd been the one to instigate their lovemaking? Did she take him for a fool?

He'd known when he accepted her offer of a coffee in her cabin that he was making a mistake, but for the first time in his life he'd ignored his own internal warnings, too caught up in the intoxication of the woman whose spell he'd slowly fallen under the longer the night had gone on to think of resisting.

Her cabin had been cosy, only a small sofa in the living space at the foot of the bed. She'd produced a bottle of vodka and two shot glasses. Her hands had trembled as she'd poured them both a slug of it. They'd downed the shots in unison and then taken their coffees to the sofa.

He'd sat facing the small television, the beats of his heart as weighty as he'd ever known them. He couldn't remember ever feeling such awareness, his body a tuning fork vibrating to the music of the woman curled beside him, her knees barely a centimetre from his thigh. The danger he'd been heading towards had rung loudly in his head. 'I should go,' he'd said. But instead of making the effort to move away from her, he'd twisted to face her.

Her head was rested against the back of the sofa, dark brown eyes on his. 'Already?' she'd sighed.

Under the soft lighting of the cabin he'd seen for the first time what beautiful smooth skin she had. His fingers had tingled to stroke her face. The warning in his head to leave immediately had grown louder.

But then she'd stroked *his* face. Just a gentle brush of the back of a finger across his jaw. His breath had caught in his throat. The vibrations of his body had thickened. Her face had inched closer to his. The backs of her fingers had then brushed down the exposed part of his neck, trailing fire over his skin. The desire in her eyes had been stark but there had been a hint of bewilderment in her stare, too, as if she was as confused as he at the thickness of the electricity crackling between them and at what her fingers were doing.

At the first whisper of her lips against his, all the

warnings in his head had been drowned in the flood of heat that had consumed him.

He severed the memories with a sharp blink.

To expect him to believe he was the only man Lena had seduced or had allowed to seduce her in the four years she'd worked here was beyond the realms of credulity. The Siopis Ice Hotel was so remote that all the staff lived in, the vast majority in special staff quarters. It was the only one of his hotels where he turned a blind eye to his staff's licentious behaviour. So long as it didn't affect their work then who was he to judge how they passed the long, dark nights when they were off shift?

He'd despised himself for those fleeting moments since their night together when his guts had coiled to imagine who the latest employee Lena had invited into her bed could be. They'd coiled to imagine *anyone* sharing her bed. Touching her. Breathing in her soft, feminine scent. Tasting her.

'I asked you a question,' he said through clenched teeth. 'If you expect me to believe I'm the father of your child, why hide it from me?' Konstantinos had amassed a fortune so vast he was regularly named as one of the top three richest Greeks. Just as believing Lena had lived like a born-again virgin for six years was beyond credulity, so, too, was believing that she wouldn't have thought she'd hit the jackpot if she'd been certain he was the father. Conceiving his child would be a lottery win for any woman, and he wasn't deluded enough not to know that greed had been the most potent mix in his lovers' desire for him.

He hadn't seen that greed in Lena's eyes, he suddenly realised, but pushed the thought away as quickly as it had formed.

Konstantinos had known since his brother's betrayal that he would never marry or settle with a permanent partner, and if he wouldn't marry or settle then he wouldn't have children. Protection against pregnancy had always been paramount when embarking on an affair…or had been until he'd been naked with a woman whose every kiss and touch had fed his hunger, and he'd realised he had no protection at hand.

'It's okay,' she'd whispered as her tongue traced the rim of his ear. 'I'm on the pill.'

Hating the thrill that ran through him at the memory, he snarled, 'You told me you were on the pill,' before she could answer his previous question.

'I was,' she replied tearfully, her eyes filling up again.

'Save your tears,' he snapped, angry with the both of them. How could he have been so stupendously stupid as to disregard the need for proper protection because in the heat of the moment he'd thought he might die if he didn't take possession of her?

But he wouldn't have died. Penetrative sex wasn't the only way to reach satisfaction. If she hadn't told him she was on the pill they would have used other means to bring each other to…

He grabbed his skull and dug his fingers into it as hard as he could. He had to stop thinking about that night.

Wiping her eyes, she leaned forward, arms

wrapped around the belly within which a baby was growing. 'Konstantinos, I'm sorry,' she said. 'You have every right to be angry with me. I was on the pill, I swear, but it was the mini-pill and you're supposed to take it at the same time every day and I was sloppy about taking it because I only used it to regulate my periods and not for protection, and at the time it didn't even cross my mind that my sloppiness would result in this, but it was entirely my fault and I am so, so sorry for that, and I'm sorry for not telling you as soon as I took the test but I was terrified of how you'd react and what you'd do, and I thought—rightly or wrongly—that it was best to wait until the baby was born before telling you because I knew you'd want a paternity test before you acknowledged our baby as yours.'

'You mean you made assumptions.'

'Of course they were assumptions but I had to do what I thought was best for me and the baby.'

'How the hell did you think you would make it to the birth without me finding out?' She wasn't obviously pregnant yet but the loose clothing she'd disguised her bump behind wouldn't hide it for much longer.

A loud rap on the door put a halt to the most excruciating conversation of Lena's life.

Konstantinos opened it. A blast of frigid air entered the cabin in the seconds it took for him to bring his luggage inside and close the door.

'I can't believe I have to stay longer in this godforsaken place,' he muttered darkly as he slung it all on the bed. He opened the larger case and glared accusingly at her. 'I'm supposed to be on my way to Australia. Magda's having to postpone all my appointments and meetings indefinitely until this mess is sorted.'

A flare of temper sneaked up on her. Lena had known he would blame her but being on the receiving end of anger that was colder than the weather outside was harder to bear than she'd imagined. 'Have you got her to put out the word for my replacement yet?'

'Don't give me ideas,' he growled before rummaging through the case.

'I'm surprised you haven't officially sacked me already. After all, you've already put Sven in charge.'

'Someone has to be in overall charge and you can't be if we're in here sorting out the mess *you've* created.'

'The mess *I* created but which you were a very willing and active participant in,' she reminded him bitterly. 'We both know you're going to sack me so why not get it over with or are you getting a kick out of prolonging my misery?'

He pulled out a pair of black, snug-fitting briefs and stepped into them. Pulling them up his legs, he bestowed her with another glare. 'So not only did you make assumptions about how I would take the news of your pregnancy, you've made assumptions that I'm going to sack you?'

'Well, that's what you did to my predecessor's predecessor.'

'*What?*' He untied the sash of his robe and irritably shrugged it off.

Suddenly confronted with his practically naked body, Lena quickly averted her eyes. 'You sacked Annika for being pregnant.'

'I did not.'

From the periphery of her vision she saw him pull on a pair of black jeans and, breaths and heartbeat quickening, had to make a concerted effort not to stare at him, hating that she *had* to make a concerted effort not to stare. How was it possible that she could be so physically aware of him when her whole life was on the cusp of being destroyed *by* him?

'I was told all about it. You called her into her office. She thought you were going to discuss her maternity leave but you sacked her on the spot for no reason.' It was Annika's dismissal that had seen Thom promoted to the general manager role and one of the receptionists promoted to Thom's role of duty manager, which in turn had created the receptionist vacancy Lena had filled. Konstantinos Siopis's sacking of the popular Annika had been a nugget of information she'd learned shortly after her arrival at the Ice Hotel and stored in the back of her mind, practically forgotten until she'd taken the pregnancy test.

'Then you were told wrong.' He dragged a black, long-sleeved top over his head and pulled it down over his muscular, thickly haired chest and abdomen. 'I sacked Annika because she allowed the lodge reception to be unmanned for two night shifts. No duty manager, no receptionist, not even a member of the housekeeping team. During one of those unmanned shifts a guest was taken ill.'

Lena's mouth dropped open in shock. 'Are you being serious?'

'Have you known me to be lauded for my jests?'

There was no reason on earth, not under the current circumstances, why this should remind her how surprised she'd been when Konstantinos had, over the course of their meal, revealed himself to actually have a sense of humour. It was a subtle, dry humour but as soon as she'd caught on to it she'd felt like a schoolgirl given the results of an incredibly hard test and learning she'd come top of the class.

It had been while grinning at something he'd said and catching the glimmer of humour in his green eyes that something had shifted in her. In practically the blink of an eye the unattractive face had taken on an endearing quality. By the end of their meal endearing had morphed into fascinating. Beauty was in the eye of the beholder and to Lena's eyes Konstantinos had become mesmerising.

It pained her that if she wasn't extremely careful, she could easily find herself mesmerised by his vampiric unattractiveness all over again.

'What happened to the guest?' she asked. It had been drilled into Lena during her induction just how important it was that both the lodge reception and The Igloo's reception always be manned. In this remote, dangerous corner of the world, anything could happen and someone needed to be available to assist in those 'anythings' at all times. The reception was always the first port of call. Everything flowed from there.

'He tripped and suffered a serious head wound walking back to his cabin at night. His wife went to the lodge for help but there was no one there.'

Her eyes widened in horror. 'No one at all?' This should not be possible.

'Now you understand why I had to dismiss her? The guest lay on the path for thirty minutes before help reached him. This was in April. The temperature was below freezing. He was lucky not to have got hypothermia.'

'I knew nothing of this.'

'I wouldn't have done either if the gentleman hadn't threatened to sue us for negligence. I paid him off and I paid Annika to go quietly, too.'

'You paid her off when she'd been grossly negligent?' If Konstantinos was telling the truth then paying Annika off made no sense. There was no reason on earth the lodge should be unmanned. There was always a duty manager and receptionist on duty at all times, plus a doctor on call and numerous other staff on hand to pitch in if needed. They were deliberately overstaffed here to stop anything like an unmanned reception ever occurring.

'I paid her off because she was pregnant.' He sat back on the armchair and locked his eyes back on her while he rolled thick socks onto his long feet. 'I didn't have to give her anything and there is not an employment judge in Europe who would have disagreed, but her baby didn't deserve to be born into hardship because of its mother's negligence, and now I would like you to explain to me how you thought you could make it to the birth without me finding out.'

It took Lena's brain a few moments to catch up with the swerve from Annika back to herself. She shook her head. 'I don't know. I was going to work as long as I could and hope you didn't get wind of it before I left.'

Socks on, he dug his elbows into his thighs and continued looking at her with the gaze of an enemy interrogator. 'You must have made some form of plan. Were you planning to leave without working your notice? Take maternity entitlement? What?'

'I wasn't stupid enough to think I could arrange maternity leave without you finding out.' Konstantinos would have to personally approve whoever was appointed to cover for her, which meant he would have definitely learned about the pregnancy before she was ready for him to know.

'Then what were you going to do? Give birth in the staff room and then demand the immediate paternity test you spoke of?'

'I don't *know*,' she repeated, her voice rising and quickening in response to his icy sarcasm. 'I just knew I needed to work for as long as I could and save as much money as I could before the baby comes because I have nothing. I have no savings, no home of my own—'

'So you want my money?'

'Absolutely.'

For a moment his expression morphed into surprise before his top lip curved in distaste. 'You admit it?'

She would not feel shamed into wanting what was best for her baby. 'My child is entitled to support from its father, and let's face it, you're not short of a bob or two.'

'Is that what this is all about? A way to extort money from me?'

'God, *no*!'

'You told me you were on the pill.'

'I told you—'

'Excuse me if I treat what you say with cynicism when you've spent months hiding the child you claim is mine. How very convenient that you fell pregnant after one night together.'

The implication that she'd either deliberately connived to get pregnant by him or was deliberately conniving to make him believe he was the father winded her.

She gazed into his cold green eyes and begged the fresh tears burning her retinas not to fall.

Were all her memories of the night they'd shared false? Had she spent months imagining the passion that had consumed them both in a whirling vortex of sensation that had left no room for thought or rationality? Had she *imagined* the depth of the shared intensity? Why else would he even consider that she'd approached their lovemaking with calculation if that passion and intensity hadn't been shared?

Somehow, that hurt far more than his scepticism of his paternity. All these months she'd comforted herself by thinking that whatever the future held for her child, at least it had been conceived with genuine passion. That she could be here now and still feel that same burning awareness for Konstantinos only made it worse.

'See?' she said shakily. 'This is why I didn't want you to know until the baby was born. You're so cynical about everything that I knew you wouldn't take my word for it being yours.'

His eyes glittered. 'Don't forget your assumption that I would sack you for it.'

'Can you blame me?'

'Yes, I can and I do, and I blame myself, too, for falling for your seduction.'

'*My* seduction?' She threw her hands in the air and shook her head with disbelief. 'So now you're rewriting history? We'd both had too much to drink, and yes, I made the first move but at least I hold my hands up and accept my responsibility for what happened but it takes two to tango, so don't even think about portraying me as some money-grabbing seductress who deliberately set out to get pregnant because if you think I ever wanted to be in the position of being a single mother with sod all money and limited emotional support then you are raving.

'All I've been trying to do these past months is build a nest egg to carry me and the baby through the birth until a paternity test confirms what I'm telling you.'

'And then what?' he sneered. 'You must have thought about what comes after. What would you like to happen? A large transfer of cash into your bank account?'

'Well, that would be nice,' she said tartly, refusing to let him see how badly his coldness was hurting her. His reaction was nothing she hadn't anticipated but living it was much worse than she'd imagined.

The pulse set off on his jaw again. 'I won't marry you,' he warned.

She reared back. 'I don't want *that.*'

Marriage hadn't even crossed her mind. Never minding that they'd spent the grand total of one night together, what woman in her right mind would want to tie herself to a man like *him*?

'I mean it, Lena. While I accept there is a strong probability that I'm the father, I will never marry you, so put the idea from your mind.'

'I just said I don't want to marry you, so get off your ego trip. You might be as rich as Midas but you're not the catch you think you are.' Jumping to her feet—she had a feeling she wouldn't be this sprightly for much longer—she folded her arms over her belly. 'Are you going to sack me?'

Now he was the one to be thrown at her swerve in the conversation. 'No, but—'

'You can stop at the *but.* If you're not going to sack me then I'm going back to work.'

'You're not going anywhere. We're talking.'

'You call going round in circles and taking verbal lumps out of each other talking?' She sucked her cheeks in as she tried even harder to keep the tears at bay, but when she continued she could hear the choke in her voice. 'We can talk tomorrow when we should both be calmer, and see if we can at least start finding common ground, but if you're not prepared to accept you're the father without a paternity test and keep coming at me as if I'm some kind of bad-faith agent then there's no point in us even doing that, and you might as well just fly off to Australia like you'd planned and we can talk properly when the baby's born.'

The way Konstantinos's elbows were digging into his thighs she thought they might bore holes into them. But he didn't say anything to stop her leaving. Not verbally. The dark tightness on his face told its own story.

# CHAPTER FIVE

An hour after Lena left his cabin, Konstantinos was still sat on the same armchair having barely moved a muscle, replaying every word they'd exchanged. Replaying Lena's hurt.

Either she was the best actress in the world or she was telling the truth and the baby was his.

Finally, he shifted position and rested his head back. Gazing up at the pitch-dark pine ceiling, he thought back twelve years to when he'd last been with Cassia. She'd looked him in the eye and told him that *of course* she still loved him and that nothing was wrong.

Deep in his guts he'd known she was lying but had chosen to believe her. Their wedding day had been fast approaching. They'd even chosen the rings and given them to Theo for safekeeping. Konstantinos had long stopped wondering if Theo wore the larger ring on his own wedding finger. Time had blurred much of the pain but not the betrayal. That still felt as fresh as the day it had happened.

There was nothing in his gut telling him Lena

was lying. If he was being truthful, his gut was telling him the opposite.

But there was an ache, too. It had been pulsing deeper even than his guts since Lena had lifted her sweater to reluctantly show him her neat, barely noticeable bump. It was a strange ache unlike the ache that always formed when he thought of her and which heated his veins just to breathe the same air as her, and it warned him more than anything of the danger of taking her word at face value.

He knew better than to take anything or anyone at face value.

Stretching his back, he got to his feet, removed his laptop from its bag, opened it, and got searching.

His eyes were gritty when he finally closed the lid.

Lena's social media presence was far more discreet than most people in their twenties. She had all the usual accounts but her privacy settings meant he couldn't access them, and so he'd searched the other staff here at the Ice Hotel and found a number for whom privacy must be an alien concept. As luck would have it, those were the staff who liked to document every aspect of their social lives and, as Konstantinos already knew, the staff here was an actively sociable crew who liked to drink and party the dark nights away when not on duty; there were many photos to go through. Lena's face was a rarity amongst them.

Pushing his laptop to one side, Konstantinos dragged his fingers through his hair. He had two choices. Hold on to his cynicism until the baby was born and then make arrangements with Lena after a paternity test confirmed what his gut was telling him. Or he could accept she was carrying his child now.

The ache deeper than his guts throbbed.

Gossip spread at the Ice Hotel quicker than the wildest wildfire but even Lena was taken aback at the avid, curious glances she kept catching from the staff. It was patently obvious the entire workforce knew Konstantinos had whisked her off to his cabin for two hours. She could guess what they thought they'd been doing.

Resolutely ignoring their curiosity, she tried her best to concentrate on her work but it was hopeless. Her head was too full of Konstantinos.

She still felt winded. More than that, felt like she'd been run over by a truck. Her insides were so squished they'd liquidised and fallen into her churning belly, and it made her burning brain swim to imagine that right this minute he could be on his way to the airport.

The thought of being on the other side of the world to him should bring relief. She'd been entirely unprepared for Konstantinos discovering the pregnancy at this point, had had no time to fortify herself against the cold opprobrium she'd known would be fired at her. She'd expected it but the reality of it hurt far more than she'd believed it could.

What if he *had* gone already? But what if he'd

stayed? She didn't know which outcome she feared the most. Or which outcome she wanted the most. It frightened her that her emotions were so heightened at the thought of either.

It made her feel wretched that she might have gotten him wrong when it came to his treatment of Annika because it was this treatment that had solidified Lena's fear of Konstantinos's reaction to her pregnancy, that he would not only deny paternity but sack her, too.

Reaching the point where she was afraid her brain would explode from the circles it was going in, she snatched her phone off her desk and made a call.

'Lena!' Thom said when he answered. 'This is a pleasant surprise.' In the background, a baby was crying. It was a sound that made her heart ache.

'Sorry to disturb you,' Lena said.

'Not at all! It's great to hear from you! How are you getting on?'

'Great, thanks,' she lied. 'How's Noomi?' she asked, referring to the crying baby whose conception had prompted Thom and his wife, Freja, to quit their jobs at the remote Ice Hotel and move to Stockholm.

After a few minutes of catching up, Lena finally found the opportunity to ask the question that had prompted her call. 'You remember Annika?'

'Sure. Why do you ask?'

'I was just wondering if you remember why she was sacked. It was before my time and all I've heard are rumours—I figured you'd know the truth.'

'She was sacked for gross negligence.' Thom proceeded to relate the exact same story Konstantinos had told her. 'What were you told?'

'I'd heard she was sacked for being pregnant.'

He snorted. 'Total rubbish but I get why people might have believed it—Mr Siopis ordered the circumstances of her sacking be kept quiet for reputational purposes. I was only told because I got her job but as far as I know, I'm the only one and I never shared it with anyone.' A strange note entered his voice. 'This is all history. Why is it concerning you now?'

'Curiosity. Anyway, thanks for satisfying it. I'll let you get on.'

There was a moment of silence before he said. 'Freja and I have a spare room if you need it. Anything you need, call us, okay?'

It was the compassion she heard in his voice and the realisation that she wasn't quite as alone here as she'd believed that had the tears spilling down her cheeks before she'd put her phone back on her desk. Burying her face in her hands, Lena let it all out.

Her tears were cathartic and once they were all purged, she felt a little better in herself.

The worst was over. Konstantinos knew about the baby. She had no control over what he would do next and to tie herself in knots about it achieved nothing. She still had a job to do and unless she wanted to give him an actual valid reason to sack her, it was best she got on with it.

Rummaging in her bag for a tissue to blow her nose in and for her emergency makeup bag, she masked the blotchiness of her cheeks as best she could with foundation and blusher, and added fresh mascara and the fawn lipstick she favoured. Reasonably happy that she no longer completely resembled the bride of Frankenstein, she woke her computer from the sleep it had fallen into and got to work.

It was 8 p.m. by the time Lena finished. Exhausted in all senses of the word, she trudged on her skis through the falling snow to her cabin at the far end of the complex where all the staff accommodation and facilities were located, set far enough from the guest cabins to make it a private—if much less plush—complex within the complex. As she passed the fir trees the guest cabins were dotted amongst, she made sure to keep her gaze fixed ahead and not peer through the trees to the super-posh cabins. She didn't know if she could bear seeing the light on in Konstantinos's. Or bear seeing it switched off.

Finally safe inside the warm confines of her cosy cabin, she thought briefly of food. She'd hardly eaten anything all day. Having no appetite, she decided to shower first and then decide if she had the energy to trundle to the staff canteen, but once she was clean and dry, fleece pyjamas on and her thick cream robe wrapped around her, she stared unenthusiastically at the ready meals stuffed in her tiny freezer. Before she could decide whether to stick macaroni cheese or spaghetti meatballs in the microwave, a sharp rap on the door made her freeze and the hairs on the nape of her neck rise.

When the door remained unopened, Konstantinos knocked again. He knew she was inside.

The handle turned, the door opened a crack, and Lena's face appeared.

His heart caught in his throat. 'Can I come in?'

She hesitated before stepping back to admit him.

Standing with her back to the wall, her dark eyes watched him warily while he went through the usual rigmarole of removing his outdoor clothing. Maybe it was because she'd clearly just showered and was dressed for bed in the un-sexiest nightwear he'd ever seen, but there was a vulnerability to her, a fragility he would never have associated with his firm-but-fair Ice Hotel general manager, as if one more blow could shatter her.

As angry as he still was with her, it sat badly with him that he was the cause of this fragility.

She waited until he'd stored his outdoor clothing in her heated cupboard before tucking her damp hair behind her ear and quietly asking, 'Does your being here mean you believe me?'

Konstantinos held her stare. *Did* he believe her? Did he genuinely believe the child in her stomach was his?

He gave a sharp nod, and immediately that he'd made the gesture, the weight that had been lodged deep inside him lifted free.

He did believe her. He did believe he was the father of Lena's child. He'd known it in his guts from the moment she'd lifted her sweater to reveal the small bump.

Her eyes closed and her shoulders slumped as if her own weight had been released. Then she straightened and, blinking rapidly, turned her face away and took the few steps to the inbuilt freezer all the staff cabins were supplied with. 'Have you eaten?'

Thrown at the question it took a moment to answer. 'No.'

Lena opened the freezer door. Her hands were shaking again. Her whole body was trembling. Konstantinos believed her. He was here. He believed her. The burst of relief had been dizzying but with it had come another welling of tears—she wouldn't have believed she had any left after the bucketload she'd cried earlier—and suddenly it had become necessary to *do* something, to keep her trembling body busy while it absorbed the shock of his unspoken admission. 'Do you want to eat with me?'

'Lena, we need to—'

'Talk,' she finished for him while keeping her gaze rooted to the meagre contents of her freezer. 'I know. And we will. Just give me a few minutes to compose myself, okay?'

'I...' He sighed but it didn't sound like an irritated sigh, more of an accepting one. 'Sure.'

'Thank you.' Blinking back more tears, she blew out a puff of air. 'Macaroni cheese or spaghetti meatballs?'

At his silence, she glanced up at him. The look he was giving her made her give a choked laugh and lightened her thumping heart a fraction. 'Not a fan of ready meals?'

He raised an eyebrow. 'I'm Greek. Ready meals are illegal there.'

She nearly asked if he was being serious but then she recognised the dryness in his voice and the glint in his eyes, and her heart lightened a little more. Whatever anger he still felt towards her, he was trying to contain it and, for the first time since she'd taken the pregnancy test, a tendril of hope unfurled that her baby's father would want to be involved in its life.

Konstantinos had watched the stress lining Lena's beautiful features melt away at his admittance of paternity and, with no makeup covering the shadows beneath her eyes, had seen the exhaustion lining them. But it was the way she'd stared into that freezer visibly trying to keep her composure that had set the wave of emotion rolling through him. And now it was the expression in her shining eyes that set another wave rolling. Such a mixture of emotions contained in them.

Lena was carrying his child. She was going to have his baby. Whether the conception had been deliberate or not he needed to accept things as they were and park his recriminations and anger.

He took a long, deep breath through his nose but it didn't help quell anything, not when it filled his lungs with the soft floral scents emanating from Lena's skin. They weren't the scents of perfume—he couldn't remember noticing her wear perfume—just the simple scents of showered cleanliness. The memories they triggered, the heat and scent of her skin underlying those scents...

He was standing far too close to her. Much closer and the swell of her breasts would brush against him.

Gritting his teeth, Konstantinos leaned back against her tiny food area to increase the gap between them.

'Go and sit down,' he ordered 'You have had two long days and you're exhausted. I'll have food delivered to us.'

Her forehead creased with confusion. Immediately, his thumbs tingled to press against the smooth skin and massage the lines away. 'We don't do cabin service for staff,' she said blankly.

He jammed his hands into his back pockets. 'We do for me.'

Lena tapped her forehead in disbelief at her own brain fade. 'Sorry,' she muttered. 'I wasn't thinking.'

Not with her brain. Konstantinos had gotten so close to her that her brain had become quite scrambled.

'Go on, sit,' he insisted. 'Take the weight off your feet. What would you like to eat?'

'Anything. You choose. I'm not fussy... But no shellfish. I'm not allowed to eat that. Bad for the baby.' While she babbled, the limited floorspace meant she had to practically shimmy past him to reach the sofa. No sooner had she slumped gratefully on it when it hit her that her lack of other seating meant Konstantinos would have to share the sofa with her. It was either that or plonk himself on the teeny bit of flooring that didn't actually have any furniture on it. If he stretched out on his side and chopped his legs off from midthigh, he might just squash into that sliver of space.

She would not allow herself to think of him sitting on her bed.

'Can you eat Arctic char?'

She turned her head back to him. He had his phone to his ear but was looking at her.

As she stuck her thumb up at him, she felt movement inside her. Her baby was awake.

While he finished giving his instructions, Lena pulled her robe open so she could rub her belly. This had become her favourite time of the day. It was as if her baby knew Mummy had finished work and woke up specially to say hello. Every day her baby's movements grew stronger.

The silence of the cabin suddenly felt very stark. Turning her head back to Konstantinos she found him staring at her stomach.

Slowly, his gaze drifted back to her face. Her heart squeezed at his expression and the longing contained in it, squeezing again to understand that this was a longing from a father to his unborn child.

Instinctively, she held a hand out to him. 'He or she's awake. Come and feel.'

He took a visible deep breath. 'You are sure?'

She nodded. Feeling her baby move inside her was the greatest blessing Lena had ever experienced in her life, and she'd often had to stop herself from imagining Konstantinos's hand on her belly marvelling at what was happening beneath the surface, sharing this most wonderful joy with him. She'd had to stop herself because her own longing had always hit the hardest then.

His throat moved before he stepped to her.

Instead of sitting beside her, he knelt before her, jaw clenched, breathing heavily.

The thuds of her heart pounded in her ears, awareness prickling her skin, but she smothered the effects as best she could.

'It doesn't bite,' she said softly when he made no effort to put his hands on her stomach or drop his gaze back to it, and then it came to her that his hesitation could be rooted in him not wanting to touch *her*.

A spasm of pain washed through her, harder to smother than the thickening awareness of him kneeling so close, his body so long his eyes were level with hers, but she smothered it enough to lift her pyjama top over her stomach and reach for his hand.

This wasn't about her. This wasn't about him. This was about their baby. Lena wanted her baby to have as close a relationship with Konstantinos as she had with her own father. Every child deserved to be loved and wanted by both its parents and until barely twenty minutes ago she hadn't dared hope her child could be loved or wanted by its father. If forging that love and want meant swallowing her hurt then that was no price to pay.

His green eyes flickered as she wrapped her much smaller fingers around his and gently pulled his hand to her stomach, then used both her hands to flatten it at the area the movement felt strongest.

The roar between Konstantinos's ears was so loud it drowned out the drum of his heart.

Being so close to Lena when he'd only just backed himself away from the warmth of her floral scent, gazing into those stunning dark brown eyes that were like melted dark chocolate, had brought the night they'd shared together crashing back into his consciousness. Remembering not the physical aspect of it all but how it had run so much deeper, right down into his core, and the very fact that he *ached* to touch her again had been the very thing that had kept him rooted to the spot.

And now his hand was flat against the swelling of her stomach, her own hands pressed against it to hold it in place, and suddenly he felt it. Movement beneath the skin.

In an instant his heart ballooned to fill every crevice of his being as finally it sank into him that this was his child. *His* child.

His other hand pressed against Lena's stomach with no thought from his confounded brain, and he sank lower, suddenly needing to look at the swelling within which his child was growing.

An unexpected grunt of awed laughter escaped his throat when the next movement happened. Sheer impulse had him slide his hands to her waist and press a kiss to the spot his baby was most active… Not just his baby but Lena's baby. Their baby.

Fingertips dug gently into his skull. He closed his

eyes at the sensation skittering over his skin before lifting his face to the woman who'd just given him the purest jolt of joy in his life.

The tenderness in Lena's eyes and the dreamy smile on her face only increased the swelling of his heart, but as he stared into those soft eyes, all the emotions consuming him began to alter. The thuds in his chest became heavier. The vim in his veins slowed to sludge. The scent of her warm body swirled into his senses and suddenly he became aware that his hands were clasped on her naked waist, that the smooth softness beneath them was her skin and as that awareness hit him, arousal thickened and he found his hands slipping around her waist to her back, his thighs rising to lift him and bring his mouth closer to the generous lips that had plagued his dreams all these months. As he closed in on her, the dreamy smile faded from her face. The tenderness in her eyes locked so tightly on his faded. There was a barely perceptible parting of her lips but it was enough for him to catch a hint of her warm, minty breath and for his senses to go into overload.

# CHAPTER SIX

THE ROAR OF blood pounding in Lena's head was so loud it drowned out everything, including her ability to think. The expression in Konstantinos's hooded eyes when he'd lifted his gaze back to hers had made her heart throb and then burst into ripples, and the detachment she'd tried so desperately to impose on herself at his closeness and the sensation of his bare hands on her skin vanished. In the blink of an eye, her lungs soaked in the warm, masculine, citrusy scent of the man whose mouth was closing in on hers and locked it inside her. Awareness danced like fire over her skin and through her veins, fingers that had unthinkingly pressed into his hair falling to his shoulders. The mesmerising vampiric face tilted almost imperceptibly, and the warmth of his coffee-laced breath seeped into her moisture-flooded mouth a fraction of a second before their lips connected. Heat flushed through every part of her. Closing her eyes, her fingers reflexively tightened on his shoulders but the kiss never went beyond a fleeting caress of the lips. With an abruptness that came from nowhere, Konstantinos jerked away like he'd had a bucket of ice thrown over him. Coldness immediately filled the vacuum made by the loss of his body heat.

Her eyes flew open.

He'd reared back on his haunches, his expression as tight as she'd ever seen it. 'Your phone,' he said in a tone that matched his expression.

Dazed at what had so nearly happened, she stared blankly at him before the ringing of her phone finally penetrated her brain.

It was her mum's ringtone.

Lena had never received a call from her mum that she didn't answer straight away, but there was no possibility of her even moving off the sofa to get it, not with Konstantinos staring at her with the look of a man who couldn't decide if he wanted to pounce on her and ravish her or plunge his teeth into her neck and suck all the life from her. His breaths were as ragged as the thuds of Lena's heart, right until he closed his eyes sharply and turned his face.

With a grace that confounded her, he rose to his feet and in a couple of strides lifted her phone from the counter above the freezer. He held it out to her wordlessly.

Still trying to pull herself out of the spell she'd been caught in, Lena straightened and took a deep breath before accepting the video call. Her mum's face filled the screen.

'There you are,' her mum said cheerfully in her native Swedish. 'I was starting to think you were ignoring…' She peered closer to the screen. 'Are you okay?'

'I'm great, thanks.' Lena twisted her angle so Konstantinos wasn't directly in her eyeline. 'It's just been a long day. How are you all?'

'All good here. The weather forecasters say we might have snow tonight.'

'Careful, you're starting to sound like a naturalised Brit.'

Her mum laughed. 'I miss the snow.'

'I know, and before I go to sleep tonight I'll do a snow chant for you.' Over more laughter, Lena asked, 'How's Heidi? Still recovering?' A moot question—her parents would have told her if Heidi's recovery from the chest infection that mercifully hadn't required hospitalisation had gone backwards in the two days since they'd last spoken. Lena had only agreed to leave England for Sweden after making her parents swear solemnly to never try to spare her worry about her sister's condition.

'She sent me to the library for audiobooks this morning.'

Ordinarily, Lena would have relaxed at this. Heidi asking for books always meant she was in a good place. With a heavy awareness of Konstantinos's attention fixed on her, there was zero chance of her relaxing into the conversation. It was hard enough thinking coherently with him sharing the same air. 'Definitely recovering well, then.'

Konstantinos had perched his backside on a tiny carved stool with a woodland scene etched on it. He was thankful it took his weight but it was so low he had to stretch his legs out, and space was so limited in the cabin that his feet were forced to rest next to Lena's. There was nowhere else for him to sit unless he sat himself beside Lena on the sofa and be forced to endure the heat of her body so close to his or, worse, sat on the bed covered in the same patchwork bedspread as the night they'd spent together. If he hadn't ordered food for them both, he would have left. A strong part of him thought he still should.

He could not believe how close he'd come to kissing her.

*Close?* Their lips had connected before her phone saved him. He'd come within a whisker of pulling her back into his arms so he could devour her properly before he'd come fully to his senses.

He could still feel the mark that brush of her lips had made against his.

Unwilling to dissect what the hell had gotten into him, he focused his attention on the video conversation being played out before him. He couldn't understand a word of what either woman was saying. He'd known Lena spoke good Swedish but had been unaware she had such fluency. One of the requirements of working at the Siopis Ice Hotel was competence in Swedish and English. Basic proficiency tests in both languages were conducted before candidates were invited to interview. Lena's Swedish... There was something sexy in her fluency. To Konstantinos's ears, it was a musical language and the way her lips moved as she spoke and her tongue wrapped around the cadences…

He shot to his feet.

Damn this cabin for being so small. Damn this country for being so cold. If they were in one of the warmer countries he favoured he'd take himself outside and when she ended her call insist she join him out there. Then he wouldn't be stuck in a space hardly bigger than his childhood bedroom breathing in all the scents of Lena. This might be a different cabin to the one they'd conceived their baby in but she'd adorned it with the same soft furnishings. She even had the same battered old teddy bear in the centre of the two pillows and the same pictures hanging on the walls. He remembered being surprised that she'd chosen artwork more suited to a small child, simple watercolour paintings of two little girls, one of them paddling in the sea, one of them making a sandcastle, and one of them playing in the snow. There was something very familiar about the snow picture that he couldn't place, and he had no idea why he should look at paintings that only the hardest-hearted person wouldn't consider 'cute' and feel nausea roiling in his guts.

Gritting his teeth, he yanked open the two cupboards above the tiny area Lena used to fix herself hot drinks and heat food. No sign of coffee, not even that instant muck… What the hell was *camomile* tea? A method of torture? His Tuscan hotel had a camomile lawn. He loathed the smell of it, only kept it because it had become a feature of the hotel.

Another voice came onto the call, interrupting his attempts to distract himself. This one caught his attention because the new voice was so different and the way Lena was conversing had changed, too, and not just because she'd switched to English. He couldn't place just how Lena's voice was different but just as looking at the pictures hanging on her pine walls made his guts roil, the way she was speaking had the same effect. There was something laboured in the voice of the new woman speaking that added to the roiling, as if every carefully chosen word was an effort to make and so the words chosen were sparse and considered.

'We have a party of Americans booked in for tomorrow's opening night,' Lena was now telling her. 'They're celebrating a fortieth birthday and birthday boy's paying for them all to freeze for the night.'

'Think…they…will…last…night?'

'I'll place my bet once I've met them.'

'Who's…that…man?' the woman in the wheelchair asked. Konstantinos only knew she was in a wheelchair because a dread-like curiosity had made his legs take him to stand at the corner of the sofa to gaze over Lena's shoulder. Next to the wheelchair was what even Konstantinos's nonmedical knowledge knew was an oxygen tank.

Lena whipped her head around at him and beseeched him with her eyes to back off. He stepped back out of view of her camera lens.

'Just a friend,' she said, giving her attention back

to the woman who looked so much like Lena that she had to be her sister.

Even though the angle Konstantinos had put himself at to keep out of the camera's range meant he didn't have a clear view, he could see the woman in the wheelchair's eyes light up.

'Don't look at me like that,' Lena scolded indignantly.

'About…time…you…had…friend.' The woman's speech might be laboured but Konstantinos heard the inverted quote marks she laced around the word *friend,* and, judging by Lena's splutter of laughter, she heard it, too.

'Your mind is filthy.'

The woman simply smiled beatifically.

'On that note, I'm going.'

The knowing smile broadened. The woman waved goodbye and then pursed her lips together.

'Love you, too,' Lena said, blowing her a kiss in return. 'Now, shoo.'

The screen on her phone went blank.

'Sorry about that,' she muttered after an awkward pause of silence, then added, 'That was my sister.'

'I guessed. She looks like you.' But a decade older than Lena's twenty-five years. 'What is wrong with her?'

Even though Lena's back was to him, he saw her tuck a lock of hair behind an ear. 'She was paralysed in a car accident six years ago.'

He said something in Greek Lena would put money on being a swear word. 'How old is she?'

'Twenty-six.'

He swore again.

The knock on the cabin door cut short a conversation Lena didn't want to have.

'I'll get it,' Konstantinos said.

She didn't argue. Her exhaustion was so great she suspected she might have trouble dragging herself off the sofa to crawl into her bed.

She didn't argue, either, when Konstantinos took charge, rooting through her cupboards for plates to serve their heat-sealed meals onto.

Sticking a cushion on her lap as a tray, she smiled her thanks when he handed her plate to her. She had a feeling the chef would cry if he saw how his usually immaculately presented food had been splattered on her plate.

'You know all the staff will be gossiping about us,' she said after they'd eaten in silence for a few minutes. At least, she'd tried to eat. It was difficult getting food down her throat with Konstantinos sitting across from her on the tiny table her mother had made for her and Heidi when they'd been little girls. She imagined it had been a long time since he'd eaten at anything but a formal dining table, never mind eating with his backside barely a foot from the floor and having to hover his plate close to his chest with one hand and so able to eat with only his fork with the other.

He stared at her meditatively as he swallowed his mouthful. While she'd managed barely a quarter of her dinner, he'd practically finished his. 'It will only get worse. It won't be long until everyone knows you're pregnant with my child.'

That tightened her throat even more.

The jaw with an abundance of black stubble tightened, too, and he said abruptly, 'What happened earlier was a mistake. I apologise.'

'Do you mean when you kissed me?'

He inclined his head.

'Do you have to keep insulting me?'

A thick black eyebrow rose.

'That's twice you've called me a mistake.'

'Lena, you are my employee.'

'Only for a few more months,' she muttered.

'We shall talk about that, but I meant—'

'What do you mean, *"We shall talk about that"*?' she interrupted, alarmed. 'You said you weren't going to sack me.'

'I'm not going to sack you but you cannot keep working here.'

'So you *are* going to sack me!'

'No!' Jaw clenched, he got to his feet and carried his plate to the sink. 'But you know as well as I do that you cannot have the baby here and I think it would be better—safer—for you and the baby if you left as soon as possible.'

'We're perfectly safe here.'

'For now, yes, but what if there are complications further along the line? The medical team and facilities here are excellent but they are not specialists in pregnancies. We need to start putting things into place now. Sven can take on your role until a permanent replacement can be appointed…' His eyes narrowed. 'You agree that you can't come back after the birth?'

She nodded miserably, not at the thought of giving up the job she loved—she'd long come to terms with that—but at the realisation that all agency she had over her own life was being lost and placed into Konstantinos's hands.

'You don't agree?'

'No, I do agree. This is no place to raise a child.' This was a frozen tourist resort in the middle of nowhere; the only Siopis hotel without childcare facilities for its staff.

'Then why are you looking like that?' he asked.

'Because I'm now in your power and it's a scary place to be.'

'You are not in my power,' he dismissed.

'Of course I am.'

'If this is about earlier then I have already apologised.'

'You think this is about our *kiss*?' she asked in disbelief.

'I woke this morning unaware you were pregnant with my child. Hours later I felt it move. The emotion of the moment got the better of me. It won't happen again.'

'Yes, I know, it was just another mistake,' she said bitterly. 'You've made your feelings towards me crystal clear. You hate me.'

'I don't hate you. I hate that you kept our baby a secret from me.'

'Because of the power you hold over me! I was always going to tell you.'

'But only when you needed my money.'

'No, when you no longer had the power to leave me destitute. One snap of your fingers and you could have made me jobless and homeless.'

'You really believed that of me?'

'Look at the way you behaved the morning after we slept together. You didn't even have the courtesy to wish me a good morning, just straight out told me it was all a mistake and then…' She snapped her fingers in the same way he could have destroyed her. Could still destroy her. 'Gone.'

The pulse on the side of his clenched jaw throbbed. 'What would you rather I'd done? Pretend I was happy to wake in your bed?'

She'd been happy to wake next to him. So very happy.

'I do not lie, Lena,' he continued. 'I despise lies.'

'You didn't have to be so cold about it.'

He rubbed the back of his head and took another deep breath before saying, 'We both crossed a line that should never have been crossed. It was better to sever it immediately.'

'Well, you did just that. You spent the night making love to me, having sex with me, *making a mistake* with me, whatever you want to call it, and then you up and left as if I was nothing but a toy you'd played with and decided was faulty.'

His vampiric face contorted with disbelief.

Her lethargy gone, Lena stood and stomped to

her teeny food area and barely resisted throwing her plate into the sink. Hands on her hips, she faced him, practically trapping him against the pine wall.

'That's *exactly* how you treated me, and you wonder why I was so scared to tell you about our baby, when you'd already made your disdain for me so clear? And then you came back five months later and made your loathing even more obvious. Until you learned about the baby you were cold and offhanded with me. I genuinely thought you were looking for a reason to sack me, and then this morning, *before* you knew about the baby, you were so keen to get away from me that you forgot your phone, so don't tell me that you only hate me for keeping our baby a secret from you. You already hated me.'

'Damn it, Lena…' He looked her square in the eyes. 'You are the only employee I have ever made this mistake with.'

She jabbed his chest. 'Stop calling me a mistake!'

He snatched her jabbing hand and held it tightly to his chest. She could feel the thumps of his heart beneath it. They matched the beats of her own thrashing heart. 'You *were* a mistake,' he snarled, green eyes swirling with dark emotion boring into her. 'It should never have happened and I have spent five months trying to forget it and forget you, and then I came back here and every time I look at you, it's all I can see. It's here in my head.' Leaning his vampiric face right into hers, he tapped the side of his skull for emphasis. 'Right here. I can't escape it. I can't escape *you*. I told you the truth the next morning that it was a mistake, and I was right. Only fools mix business with pleasure so that made me the fool who had to put the most incredible night of my life out of my mind and forget about it. God knows I've tried but I can't forget, and if I've been cold with you it's because sharing the same air as you—'

Lena's mouth suddenly attached itself to his. It came without thought or reason, her body taking full control for a swift, clumsy kiss that had, for one fleeting instant, felt as necessary as taking her next breath.

Konstantinos froze. A short beat later Lena froze, too, in horror at what she was doing, and reared away from him. Brain burning, frightened to look at him, heart racing and blood pumping frantically, she pulled her hand free from his and quickly edged away from him, already planning to lock herself in the bathroom until her mortification had passed when his large hand snatched at her wrist and he yanked her back to him.

An arm snaked tightly around her waist, crushing her against him and then his mouth came crashing down.

With a moan that seemed to come from the very core of her being, Lena melted into Konstantinos and the dark power of his kiss. Lips fused, tongues entwined, arms wrapped around each other, until every inch of their bodies that could be flush pressed together and every single tendril of emotion and pleasure she'd experienced in his arms roared back to life.

This…this was what had clung like a cloud to her all these months. The sheer headiness she'd found in the taste of his passionate kisses and the scent of his skin and the thrills of his touch. All of her senses responded to him, as if Konstantinos Siopis had been specially created for her sensory delectation, and being with him now, caught in the hot fever that had captured them that night in an explosion of hedonistic lust…oh, it was the most incredible feeling in the world.

Hot, sticky desire pulsed through Konstantinos, the arousal he'd kept under such tight control unleashed, urgent, scorching him. Pressing Lena against the wall, he devoured her mouth, her hot sweetness feeding his hunger, thrills ravaging him. Other than their devouring faces, not an inch of flesh touched through the thick layers they wore, but the heat from their crushed bodies was as consuming as if they were naked.

It was a heat like no other. The way he reacted to Lena was like with no other. For five months the night they'd spent together had been a living memory constantly springing free from the reinforced crate he kept jamming it into. He'd been unable to enjoy even the simple pleasure of a glass of wine without conjuring Lena's smile as she drank her own wine, unable to see the colour red without the image of unbuttoning her red blouse flashing into his mind. Damn it, even seeing the delivery of ice at one of his hotels had immediately made him think of her, which alone was enough for his loins to heat.

That was the worst part of it. It was impossible to think of her and the night they'd spent together without the accompanying tell-tale signs of arousal. Hundreds, often thousands, of miles of distance between them, differing time zones and climates and all it took was for him to close his eyes and he could feel her nails scraping over his naked back.

Breaths ragged and painful, he broke the fusion of their mouths and stared at her flushed, beautiful face with a heart that had swollen large enough to choke him. When he gazed into her desire-drugged eyes it came to him that much of the anger he'd been carrying since their night together had dissipated. Every part of him throbbed with desire but an invisible weight he'd barely noticed himself carrying had lifted.

'Please don't tell me that was a mistake,' she whispered, resting her head back against the wall.

His swollen heart clenched. 'That might have been my biggest mistake.'

She shook her head. 'Don't.'

With a groan, he rested his forehead to hers. 'Lena, I don't want there to be lies between us. There have been too many already.'

'I know. And I'm sorry.'

To his surprise, he believed her. He disentangled his arms so he could run his fingers through her hair and clasp the back of her head. 'I have spent all this time trying to forget our night together and now I learn you are having my baby, and I have to navigate a future where you are going to be in my life for the rest of my life and I don't even know how the hell to begin navigating it.'

She gave a wobbly smile. 'I don't know how to navigate it, either.'

He stared into her beautiful eyes and felt another clenching of his heart. 'I promise I will support you financially and in any other way I can, and be a father to our child as best I can, but that is as much as I can promise.'

She gave another wobbly smile and nodded. 'The only promise I want from you is the promise to always put our child first.'

The clenching in his chest tightened to a point. Resisting the growing urge to kiss her again, he bowed his head and stepped away from her completely, making his way to the cupboard he'd stored his outdoor clothing in. It was time to get out of this suffocating cabin and Lena's overwhelming presence. 'I give you my word.'

# CHAPTER SEVEN

THE NEXT MORNING Lena ski-walked past Father Christmas ski-walking to his newly opened grotto, and grinned. The Siopis Ice Hotel didn't cater to children, but in December the snow and the atmosphere of the place turned many of their guests into big kids.

At the lodge she carefully removed her skis and placed them in the staff rack, then shook off the layer of snow that had fallen thick and fast during the slow journey from her cabin, and stepped inside. The warmth was welcome as was the brightness of the internal daylight-mimicking lights. She hoped the forecast of blizzards the next day proved wrong. There was nothing worse than making your way around the complex with zero visibility. Occasionally, the blizzards became bad enough that planes at the local airport couldn't land or take off.

As usual, the first thing she did once settled in her office was check their incoming and outgoing guests' flight status. No flights tomorrow, so if the predicted blizzard did hit, they wouldn't have to scramble for extra accommodation if those supposed to leave were trapped.

Busying herself firing off emails and messages to all the various teams involved in getting guests wherever they needed to be and ensuring everyone was prepared with the necessary bad weather contingency plans, it was the sudden plummet of Lena's stomach that alerted her to her office door being pushed open. She lifted her gaze to find Konstantinos stepping over the threshold.

The long, lean frame wrapped in the usual dapper dark suit and the darkly unattractive freshly shaved face that made her heart swell so greatly loomed over her desk before he sank into the visitor chair opposite her.

The greeting she'd found for everyone else she'd seen that morning refused to form for him. Her throat had closed too tightly.

His strong throat moved before he broke the silence. 'All okay?'

She nodded the lie she couldn't form verbally. Truth was, Lena was far from okay. Her emotions were all over the place. She couldn't make sense of any of it. Couldn't make sense of why, when Konstantinos had left her cabin so soon after the passion between them had erupted, she'd had to clamp her lips together to stop herself begging him to stay. Or make sense of why, during the long, dark night, she'd spent the many lonely hours fighting the yearning to call him, just to hear his voice.

She must be a masochist. That was the only ex-

planation. Or her hormones were more bonkers than
she'd given them credit for. Probably a combination
of the two and all aggravated by that stupid, heav-
enly, passionate kiss, a kiss her cheeks kept flaming
to remember that *she'd* instigated.

She was definitely a masochist. How else to explain why her reaction to a man angrily reeling off
the reasons why sleeping with her had been a mistake was to stop him talking with a kiss?

It didn't matter that he'd pulled her back to him
or that he'd been the one to envelop her in his arms
and hold her so tightly while devouring her mouth.
Compounding his mistake. If she hadn't made the
first move, he wouldn't have made the second.

What was *wrong* with her? She'd made all the
running the night they'd shared together, inviting
him into her cabin, being openly dismayed when
he said he should leave, angling her body closer to
his, kissing him… It had all been *her*. She'd started
it! He'd responded but she'd been the instigator, and
she had no doubt that if she hadn't, nothing would
have happened. Konstantinos would never have made
the first move. And now she knew she couldn't even
partially blame her actions that night on all the wine
because she'd done it all again stone-cold sober.

For whatever reason, being close to Konstantinos
seemed to cast a spell on her and make her act like
a teenager with a crush. She accepted that she did
have a crush on him—be a bit silly to deny something so obvious—but she wasn't a teenager, she
was an adult, and it beggared belief that she could

be mooning over a man who'd treated her like dirt after their one night together and might as well have spelt it out in neon lights that he wasn't interested in a relationship.

*She* shouldn't be interested in a relationship, either. She wasn't! She'd had no interest in relationships since the accident and chances were, if not for the baby, she wouldn't be entertaining any of these thoughts. But she *was* having his baby. A part of Konstantinos Siopis was growing inside her, so surely it would be more worrying if she wasn't entertaining relationship thoughts about the father of her child? Because didn't it make sense to at least try and see, for their baby's sake, if a relationship between them could work?

Oh, this was all so confusing.

It would be easier if he felt nothing for her. Even simple hate would be easier to deal with. It was his desire for her that added such toxicity to her confusion. Konstantinos had such detachment over his emotions that he found it easy to separate his desire from his head. Lena could only hope time would make that same detachment easy for her to find, too.

'I have rearranged my schedule,' he told her with that hateful vocal detachment. 'We shall stay here for another week. That will give us time to find a temporary replacement for you and get things in motion for a permanent replacement. I think Sven is well qualified to take the role temporarily—do you agree?'

'You want me to leave in a week?'

'We have already agreed that it is best you leave sooner rather than later.'

'I didn't think you meant that quickly.' She finally plucked up the courage to look him in the eye. Her heart flipped over to see the blaze roaring from them, completely belying his external aloofness, making it even harder for her to concentrate and get her words out. 'I don't have anywhere to go. My parents only have a sofa I can sleep on, which was fine when I wasn't pregnant, and my grandmother's cabin near Trollarudden isn't habitable. There's nowhere else for me to go.'

Konstantinos sounded out the unfamiliar word. 'Trollarudden?'

'Near Borlange?'

He shook his head. He'd never heard of it.

'It's hundreds of miles south from here.'

Everything was hundreds of miles south of here. 'In Sweden?'

'Yes. My mother's Swedish.'

'Ah.' That explained a lot.

'We spent our childhood summers at my grandmother's cabin here. My parents are teachers so had the same long holidays we had. Mormor—my grandmother—died when I was sixteen. My parents sold her house but we kept the cabin.' She grimaced. 'We always meant to make good use of it but the accident changed everything. I went to check it all over a couple of years ago and it's falling into ruin.'

'The accident…do you mean the one that paralysed your sister?'

She nodded.

'Do they know you're pregnant?'

'No.'

'Why not? I got the impression from your video call that you are a close family.'

'We are.' She sighed. 'I was going to tell them on my next visit home—I don't imagine I'll be able to hide it by then.'

'Why would you want to hide it from them?'

'I don't, I just thought it better to wait until nearer the birth. They're in no position to help me and they have enough to worry about with Heidi. She needs twenty-four-hour care. The last thing they needed was to spend nine months worrying about me, too.'

Though he would prefer not to look too closely at Lena's face and have to deal with the accompanying violent roll in his guts and the deepening of the awareness tormenting him just to share four walls with her, Konstantinos needed to see for himself if she was telling the truth or simply feeding him a line to make herself sound more in need of help than she actually was. He couldn't shake the nagging voice in the back of his mind that she'd deliberately seduced him for the sole reason of conceiving his child.

There was no need for her to play games. Deliberate conception or not, it made no difference to him if she had an army of family and friends offering their help; her child was his child. His responsibility. That made Lena's comfort and safety his responsibility, too.

Allowing himself to fully gaze into the dark

brown eyes made his heart clench tightly. Too tightly. Made him remember the look on her flushed face last night when she'd suddenly pressed her lips to his.

*Theos*, she'd backed off as if she'd been scalded. *He'd* been the one to lose control of the situation. Him. What the hell had he been thinking, pulling her into his arms like that when he damned well knew to keep a physical distance between them?

He gritted his teeth in an ineffectual attempt to counter the throbs of awareness burning beneath his skin and lowered his stare to her desk. Lena had placed a miniature Christmas tree on it and wrapped tinsel around the framed photograph next to her monitor. He'd seen the photo before, only yesterday morning when he'd sat where Lena now sat, plotting his quick escape from this freezing hellhole. Those last minutes before he'd learned the secret she'd been hiding from him.

Twisting the photo round, he looked again at the two small girls—Lena and her sister—playing in the snow, and suddenly it came to him why the watercolour painting on her cabin wall had seemed so familiar. 'This is the photograph used to create the painting in your cabin?'

'Yes. My mother painted it. She often used photos as inspiration for her art.'

'Does she still paint?'

'Rarely.'

The sadness in her voice made him look back at her.

'Heidi's health issues are incredibly complex. She

sustained such damage...' She trailed off with another deep sigh before her shoulders rose briskly and a note entered her voice to match. 'Mum and Dad share her care. They both reduced their work to part-time so one of them is always around for her. It doesn't leave much time for anything else.'

'Then why have you spent years here, thousands of miles from them, and not with them, helping with their burden?'

The anger that darkened and pinched her face was instantaneous. Pushing herself forward on the desk, she spoke with quiet venom. 'Heidi is not a *burden*. She is my sister and their daughter and we love her and would do anything for her, and I would thank you not to cast judgement on choices made that you know *nothing* about.'

'I wasn't making a judgement,' he refuted coolly. 'I was making an observation.'

'An observation cast like a judgement.'

He'd hit on a weak spot there, he thought. Was it guilt making her react so defensively?

At this thought, a pang of guilt punched through him. The evidence of Lena's love for her family and their love for her was everywhere. The photo of the two Weir girls playing in the snow was one of three photos in her office of her family. Her cabin was stuffed with family photos that he'd deliberately avoided looking at because it was easier to try and banish her from his mind if she was a caricature in his mind and not a flesh and blood woman with feelings.

He'd made his judgemental observation deliberately. With the intention of hurting her. And he'd succeeded.

Damn it, it wasn't Lena's fault he reacted so viscerally to her and that he was sitting in this confined office—*everywhere* in this hellscape was confined—fighting with every breath in his body not to pull her to him for a taste of her sweet headiness. He shouldn't punish her for his desire and his failure to control it.

'Do you want to be based near them when the baby comes?' he asked, making an effort to neuter the atmosphere he'd created. When her pinched features remained stony, he added, 'Everything is changing, Lena, and you will need a home. Given the choice, would you prefer to be close to your family or somewhere else?'

Holding his stare a moment longer, she drew her chest slowly off the desk and leaned back in her chair. Her expression now wary, she said, 'My choice would be to live close to my family.'

'Then I shall make it happen. Email me their address and I will get my people on it.'

'On it?'

'To find a suitable home for you and the baby close to your family. You get the final choice and the contracts will be made in your name. The home will be yours.'

Her mouth dropped open. 'That is… Are you sure?'

'Of course,' he dismissed. 'But I am not a miracle

worker. It might take a month or two before you are able to move into it. I have a penthouse in London you can use until then.'

She shook her head as if clearing water from her ears but the wariness remained. 'That is very kind and generous of you.'

'I am a kind and generous man,' he said drolly.

She gave a sudden snort of laughter that made her shoulders shake and finally removed the last trace of her bristling anger.

Konstantinos had no idea why it made him feel so ridiculously pleased to hear that laughter again and why the softness returning to her eyes should ease the pressure that upsetting her had put on his chest, and then he remembered how hearing that laugh and seeing that softness during their celebratory meal had gone a long way into seducing him. It was a rare person who drew the humour out in him, a rarer person still who *got* it and by extension got him. Lena's gift that night—whether genuine or not—had been to make him feel that she'd looked beneath the ugly but wealthy exterior and seen the beating heart of the man, and that she'd liked what she'd seen. It had been an incredibly powerful aphrodisiac that had intoxicated him and drawn him into making the biggest mistake of his life because, unlike his usual dispassionate affairs, the remnants of their lovemaking had never left him.

'All I ask in return is that you spend Christmas with my family.'

The dark eyes that had widened with such pas-

sionate surprise at her first climax with him came
close to popping out of her head. 'You've told your
family about the baby?'

'Yes.' Like ripping a sticking plaster off in one go,
he'd known it was best to get it over and done with
and just tell them.

'How did they take it?'

'Very well.'

The wariness returned but this time underlined
by fear rather than anger. 'You told them the circumstances?'

'Only that we are not in a relationship, but do not
let that worry you. Family is everything to my parents and they want to welcome you into ours.'

'Really?

'To them, this is a blessing. They long ago gave
up hope I would have children.' Only in the past few
years had they stopped asking if he'd 'met' anyone. It
had taken him a long time to control his anger at their
bewilderment in his absolute refusal to even consider
finding a partner. They'd been there. They knew the
effect Theo's betrayal had had on him. 'They want to
meet you. They are like children themselves when it
comes to Christmas and it would bring them much
joy to involve you in our celebrations of it. That isn't
a problem for you, is it?' he added when Lena didn't
respond. 'You couldn't have made plans to celebrate
it with your family. You were supposed to be working the period here.'

'It's not a problem, no,' she said slowly. 'You've

just taken me by surprise. I don't think I'd even considered that you had parents.'

'How else did you think I came to be here? Did you think I was grown on a Petri dish?'

The grin that spread over her face at this zinged through the air between them and injected another dangerous dose of warmth into his veins.

'I had wondered,' she said with a snigger. 'I take it this will be their first grandchild?'

'Their third.'

'I don't know why but I was always under the impression you were an only child,' she mused. 'How old are they?'

'My nephews? Seven and three.'

'That will be nice for our child. We have cousins from my dad's side and it was always such a laugh when we got together as kids. We adored seeing them.'

'That will not happen for our child. I have not seen my brother in twelve years.'

That shocked her, he could see.

This was not a conversation Konstantinos wished to have but now it was here, he could see the necessity in telling her about it. Lena would discover the reasons for his estrangement from his brother at some point. Better to have it out in the open now. Better she understood, too, why she could never be more to him than his child's mother, and from the tempest of emotions thrashing through him just to sit across a desk from her, he knew he needed to remind himself, too, before the temptation to act on his emotions got the better of him again. Remind himself exactly why he would never commit himself to a woman again or trust their motives.

'His wife was supposed to be my wife.'

Her smooth brow creased. *'What...?'*

'My brother stole my fiancée from me.'

All the lightness on Lena's features vanished.

Keeping tight control of his own features, he said, 'I'd known Cassia all my life. She went to my school and worked in my parents' restaurant at weekends. I worshipped the ground she walked on but she never looked twice at me, not until I turned twenty.' He tapped his bent, overlong nose and added sardonically, 'None of the girls ever looked twice at me.'

The coldness that seeped into Lena's veins as he spoke sent the most horrible shiver coiling up her spine.

'She went to university but quit after a year and started working full-time for us. When she finally agreed to a date, I thought all my birthdays had come at once. She was my first lover. I hoped she would be my only lover. When she agreed to marry me, I thought I was the luckiest man alive. I was never ambitious until we got together. The family restaurant brought in enough money for us to have a decent life but in my eyes, Cassia was a princess, and princesses deserved the best of everything. I wanted to give her the world. I convinced my parents to take out a mortgage on the restaurant so I could buy my own. From that, I bought another and then another, and then I bought my first hotel. I wasn't rich like

I am now, not by any means, but I worked hard and was turning over a decent profit. I believed Cassia and I would have the comfortable life we'd dreamed of with enough money to travel to exotic parts of the world and raise a family. What I didn't know was that while I was working hard to build our comfortable life, she'd started screwing my brother.'

Lena was finding it hard to breathe. She didn't know what was worse, what Konstantinos was revealing or the absolute dispassion in the way he was telling it. No, she did know what the worst part was—the fire in his eyes. The warnings being fired at her.

He was telling her all this for a reason.

'Two weeks before our wedding day she finally found the guts to tell me the truth. She didn't love me. She'd never loved me. She only agreed to that first date to make Theo jealous. It was my brother she really wanted. Not me.'

Lena covered her mouth in horror. She wished she could cover her ears, too. This was horrendous. Just horrendous. The kind of betrayal that must rip a man's heart out.

He grunted a laugh that landed on her ears like nails on a chalkboard. 'And Theo wanted her, too. I knew he thought Cassia attractive—he was always joking about me punching above my weight with her—but I never dreamed he would act on it and betray me like that.'

'I'm so sorry,' she whispered hoarsely.

'What for? If they hadn't betrayed me I wouldn't

have needed to find solace in my work. I wouldn't have built this empire.' He gave another of those awful laughs. 'I should have seen it coming. Theo is movie-star handsome. Why would the princess want the ugly brother when she could have the handsome prince?'

'You are not ugly,' she said vehemently, wishing she could teleport herself to Kos and scratch the eyes out of the two people who'd behaved so cruelly and caused such devastation.

Leaning over her desk, he eyeballed her. 'The mirror does not lie. If I wasn't rich, you wouldn't have looked twice at me. None of the women I've been intimate with would have.'

He shoved his chair back before she could even think of a response to his hurtful accusation. When he next looked at her, there was a gentler expression on his face. 'I am sorry if I sound bitter. I haven't spoken about Theo and Cassia in many years but it is only right you know about it, and hear it from me and not some gossip in Kos. Now you will have to excuse me—I have video calls to make. Tell Sven to join us in the meeting room in an hour so we can start on the transition process.'

He swept out of the office and closed the door behind him without looking back at her.

# CHAPTER EIGHT

'I UNDERSTAND THERE is a blizzard and storm expected later today,' Konstantinos said as a form of greeting when he stepped into Lena's office the next morning.

Even though he hadn't told her to expect him this early, she greeted him with a cordial smile. 'There is a chance of it. It might miss us.'

He took a seat on the visitors' chair. 'Have you put the contingencies in place?'

'Yes.'

'It has been a few years since I've touched base on this. Explain them to me.'

She rolled her chair back until it touched the wall and then spoke in polite, professional detail about how they ensured guest and staff safety in extreme weather.

'Is Sven aware of the procedures?'

'All the staff are aware. It is part of our induction and we do ongoing training, too, to keep it fresh in people's minds.'

Now he remembered one of the things that had impressed him when he'd interviewed Lena for the general manager's role was her suggestion that the ongoing training be increased. She'd implemented it within days of starting the job.

'What time is he due?' In their meeting with Sven the day before, one conducted in an atmosphere as cordial as the one they were having now, Konstantinos and Lena had discussed the transition process and Konstantinos's expectations of him for when he took over the role. The meeting had been cut short when Konstantinos needed to video call with his directors. He'd left Lena to arrange a time to continue it for that day.

'In two hours.'

'Good. That gives you time to look at the homes my people have shortlisted for you.'

Not by a flicker did she react in any way that could be construed as delight or pleasure, her features retaining their amiability, her tone remaining polite. 'That is wonderful, thank you, but I will have to look at them later—I'm due to give Jocasta her appraisal in ten minutes.'

'Should Sven not sit in on it so he can see how they're conducted?'

'We've already agreed he will sit in on Mikhail's appraisal at four.'

She didn't miss a trick. Of all his managers, she was by far the most thorough and conscientious. His hotel's loss was his baby's gain, a thought that gave him no satisfaction whatsoever. Konstantinos had felt out of sorts since he'd woken at what would have been the crack of dawn in any normal part of the

# "One Minute" Survey

## You get up to **FOUR** books <u>and</u> a Mystery Gift...

### ABSOLUTELY FREE!

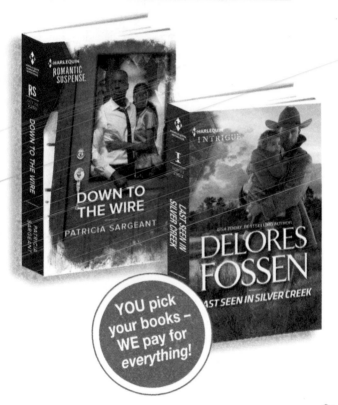

See inside for details.

Dear Reader,

Your opinions are important to us. So if you'll participate in our fast and free "One Minute" Survey, YOU can pick up to four wonderful books that WE pay for when you try the Harlequin Reader Service!

As a leading publisher of women's fiction, we'd love to hear from you. That's why we promise to reward you for completing our survey.

IMPORTANT: Please complete the survey and return it. We'll send your Free Books and a Free Mystery Gift right away. And we pay for shipping and handling too!

*← We pay for EVERYTHING!*

Try **Harlequin® Romantic Suspense** and get 2 books featuring heart-racing page-turners with unexpected plot twists and irresistible chemistry that will keep you guessing to the very end.

Try **Harlequin Intrigue® Larger-Print** and get 2 books featuring action-packed stories that will keep you on the edge of your seat. Solve the crime and deliver justice at all costs.

**Or TRY BOTH!**

Thank you again for participating in our "One Minute" Survey. It really takes just a minute (or less) to complete the survey... and your free books and gift will be well worth it!

If you continue with your subscription, you can look forward to curated monthly shipments of brand-new books from your selected series, always at a discount off the cover price! Plus you can cancel any time. So don't miss out, return your One Minute Survey today to get your Free books.

*Pam Powers*

# "One Minute" Survey

## GET YOUR FREE BOOKS AND A FREE GIFT!

✓ Complete this Survey ✓ Return this survey

▶ DETACH AND MAIL CARD TODAY! ▶

**1** Do you try to find time to read every day?
☐ YES ☐ NO

**2** Do you prefer stories with suspensful storylines?
☐ YES ☐ NO

**3** Do you enjoy having books delivered to your home?
☐ YES ☐ NO

**4** Do you share your favorite books with friends?
☐ YES ☐ NO

**YES!** I have completed the above "One Minute" Survey. Please send me m
Free Books and a Free Mystery Gift (worth over \$20 retail). I understand that I an
under no obligation to buy anything, as explained on the back of this card.

☐ **Harlequin® Romantic Suspense** 240/340 CTI G2AD

☐ **Harlequin Intrigue® Larger-Print** 199/399 CTI G2AD

☐ **BOTH** 240/340 & 199/399 CTI G2AE

FIRST NAME

LAST NAME

ADDRESS

APT.#

CITY

STATE/PROV.

ZIP/POSTAL CODE

EMAIL ☐ Please check this box if you would like to receive newsletters and promotional emails from Harlequin Enterprises ULC and its affiliates. You can unsubscribe anytime.

HI/HRS-1123-OM

world. His sleep had been abysmal, something he blamed Lena for.

Their conversation about his brother and Cassia's betrayal had had the desired effect. Any hint of emotional turbulence from Lena had been extinguished. She'd understood his unspoken message, that much was clear. What was not clear was why he was unable to get his own body to compute the message. Her body language was everything he wanted, not a hint of the expressive emotions that fed into his veins, not even during the meal they'd shared at the Brasserie last night when she'd acted as if she was dining with a business acquaintance. It was how she should have acted during their celebratory meal five months ago, he thought grimly. How *he* should have acted, too. And then he'd walked her back to her cabin like a gentleman should, the beats of his heart getting stronger the closer they'd gotten to it, his nerve endings tingling even as he mentally prepared the rebuffs he would make when she invited him inside, only to reach her door and be wished a brisk good-night.

'I shall sit in on Jocasta's appraisal,' he decided, folding his arms across his chest. He would have to deal with Lena for the rest of his life. Practice would make perfect his determination to rid himself of this physical infatuation he seemed to have developed for her.

If Lena was perturbed at this declaration, she didn't show it. 'In that case, I will have extra pastries brought in.'

He raised an eyebrow. 'You provide refreshments when you do appraisals?'

'I find it makes for a nicer atmosphere and allows them to relax.'

'An appraisal of your staff's work should be conducted professionally, not as if you're conducting a tea party.'

'It is conducted professionally, as you will discover when Jocasta gets here.'

'Professionally with pastries?'

'I prefer the carrot to the stick approach. It creates a feeling of openness.'

'That sounds like psychobabble.'

She shrugged. 'It's my way of working.'

'Because you dislike confrontation?'

'I dislike *unnecessary* confrontation,' she corrected, the slightest hint of steel sounding in her calm voice. 'I have appraised a dozen staff since I took the role and sent the full reports to you. If you had a problem with them, you should have told me.'

She had him there, but he was saved from wondering too deeply why he was doing his best to pick fault with her—unnecessary fault at that, seeing as she'd no longer be his employee in four days—by a tap on the door.

Lena welcomed an early Jocasta inside, called out to her assistant for the refreshments to be brought in, and prayed for the strength not to punch Konstantinos in the face. She had the distinct impression he was deliberately trying to find fault with her, although to what end she couldn't begin to imagine.

She was doing her best. The message he'd given her when relating his brother and fiancée's betrayal had been received and understood. When he said he didn't do relationships and that she would only ever be the mother of his child to him, he meant it. Nothing more needed to be said about it, not by either of them. His accusation that she'd only slept with him because of his wealth sealed it. That he still had such a low opinion of her and that the most incredible night of her life was so diminished in his mind hurt immeasurably, but she couldn't defend herself because to do so would only dredge it all up again.

She wished he'd delivered his message when her time here in Sweden was done, not when she still had to suffer four days of his unceasing presence and had to pretend she felt nothing. She was proud, though, that when he'd walked her back to her chalet after their polite dinner together where they had made a tentative plan on how best to co-parent their child, she'd let herself in without giving in to the plaintive yearning to invite him inside; proud, too, that when he'd appeared in her office that morning she'd smothered the swirl of emotions playing havoc inside her to greet him with a smile.

Her crush needed to be kept under lock and key. The emotions Konstantinos created in her needed to be contained. It was the only way she could get through the next few days.

Lena had only just stepped out of the shower when her phone rang, a frantic Katya informing her that

Niels, the night duty manager at The Igloo, had taken sick.

'Okay,' Lena said, 'let me make some calls. I'll have a replacement with you shortly. Any other problems I should know about?'

'No, but the way the snow's falling, it looks like the blizzard is coming our way after all.'

Looking out her window, she saw what Katya meant. Lena's hope as the day had gone on that heavy snow was the worst they would get looked to have been premature.

Five minutes later and she called Katya back to tell her she was on her way. Rachel, a currently off-shift duty manager, was going to take Niels's shift but, as Rachel had not yet had her dinner, Lena had offered to cover the first hour so Rachel could get some food in her. It also gave her an excellent excuse to message Konstantinos and get out of the meal with him she'd been unable to think of a spontaneous excuse to refuse.

Duty manager at Igloo sick. Need to cover so won't be able to make dinner.

She'd grab something to eat at the staff canteen on her way back, she thought as she quickly donned her layers and put her snowsuit on. Before setting out, she took the precaution of changing the batteries of both her head torch and her walkie-talkie. Out here, you could never be too careful.

Lena set off, her thoughts automatically taking her to Konstantinos.

She'd had no respite from him until she'd turned her computer off at six. The whole working day, he'd been there, tormenting her with his presence, filling her office and the corridors of the lodge with his citrusy cologne. Even his stubble had taunted her, steadily thickening as the day had gone on, reminding her of the pleasurable pain of it scratching against her skin.

The emotional distance she'd tried to impose had made no difference, she thought miserably as she carefully navigated her way through worsening visibility to the complex's main road. Konstantinos only had to walk into a room for flames to flicker inside her and her resolutions to flounder. Oh, she was *pathetic*.

Four more days and then she'd be out of here. He would install her in his London penthouse, a thirty-minute train ride from her family, and then off he'd pop to wherever was next on his itinerary and she'd get a couple of weeks respite from him. She'd have to suffer his presence over Christmas but it was only for a few days. After that, there was no reason to imagine she'd have to deal with him at all in person until the baby came. That would be more than enough time to get her stupid wayward feelings for him in order.

The falling snow was impenetrable but Konstantinos grimly held his steady course until The Igloo's reception appeared, not as a structure but as a hazy block of light. Abandoning the snowmobile he'd had to fight the impulse not to ride at full speed, he bowed his head against the whiteout and crashed his way through the reception door.

The shock on Lena's face at his appearance would have been amusing if her reckless actions hadn't snuffed any humour out of him. He'd half expected to arrive here and find that she hadn't turned up, that she was lost in the blizzard.

'What are you doing here?' she asked.

He stamped more snow off his boots, uncaring of the pile of slush he was creating around him, and ripped his gloves off. 'The very question I wish to ask of you.'

Her message cancelling their dinner date had pinged into his phone while he was taking a bath. As he'd been taking a screen break, it had gone unread for forty minutes.

She looked around the horseshoe reception desk she was currently standing behind with a bemused expression. 'I'm covering for Niels until Rachel gets here. She's on her way.'

'So that's two reckless members of staff I pay wages to.'

That took her aback. 'What do you mean by that?'

'Going out in this abysmal weather is the height of recklessness.'

'Not as reckless as leaving The Igloo short staffed,' she countered calmly. 'Niels is ill. Besides, as we discussed just this morning, we're trained to cope with the weather.'

He jabbed a finger in the direction of the door. 'That is not *weather*. That is hell.'

'We're near the Arctic Circle. We get snow. We deal with it. That's what you pay us good money for.'

'That is more than snow.'

'Yes, it's a blizzard. It's unfortunate but, as I said, we deal with it.'

Her serenity was as infuriating as her irresponsible actions. After stomping over to the reception desk, he slammed his hands on it. 'Deal with it? Lena, you are five months pregnant.'

'And?'

'Don't be obtuse,' he snarled. 'I cannot believe you would endanger yourself and our child like this.'

The calm vanished. Angry colour staining her face, she slammed her hands down on the other side of the desk in imitation of him and leaned forward, bringing her face close to his. 'Excuse me, *buster*, but that is insulting poppycock. The snow wasn't as heavy as this when I set off, and even if it was, I've lived here for four years and can ski-walk the route with my eyes closed. I have never had the slightest weather-related accident here because I treat the weather conditions with respect and understand my own limits. I was well wrapped up and had taken every precaution—we *all* take every precaution. I'm not an invalid and my bump isn't big enough yet to cause me balance problems, and for you to even suggest I would endanger our child is so insulting it makes me want to be sick, so go and take your judgement and stick it where the sun doesn't shine!'

If the reception door hadn't opened and a person, so thickly covered in snow they could be mistaken for a yeti, thrown themselves inside, Konstantinos thought he might have exploded with rage.

'Sorry, Lena,' the woman said as she shook her hood off. 'It's *awful* out there. I couldn't see what I was doing to shake the snow off outside...' She suddenly clocked Konstantinos and squeaked, 'Mr Siopis!'

He nodded a terse greeting.

Glaring at Konstantinos before dragging a smile to her face for Rachel, Lena hurried over to her, thankful for the excuse to get away from him. That he had the nerve to criticise her for doing her job was beyond credulity.

'Here, let me help you out of that.' Konstantinos could jolly well freeze in his snowsuit for all she cared. 'Is it really that bad out there?'

'I couldn't see a thing. If we didn't have the guide ropes I'd have lost my way.'

She looked out the window. Rachel was not exaggerating. To think Konstantinos had made the journey on a snowmobile—she'd seen the glare of its lights barely a minute before he'd stormed inside—only ratcheted up her fury at his sanctimony and hypocrisy. He might own the place but he didn't know the landscape. He'd had none of the training she and all the other staff undertook. The idiot could easily have gotten lost or stuck in a snowdrift. She'd bet he didn't even have an emergency walkie-talkie on him.

'If I'd known it was going to get this bad I'd have told you to stay in your cabin and done the shift myself,' she said, trying hard not to let her fury at Konstantinos sound out in her words to Rachel.

'Well, I'm here now so you can go off if—'

'She is not going anywhere until the blizzard clears,' Konstantinos interrupted rudely, making Rachel blink with surprise and Lena openly glare at him again. It felt like she'd spent the whole day on the defensive against his subtle sniping and now he couldn't even be bothered to be subtle about it and she'd had enough. If he could be rude to her then she could be rude back. What was he going to do about it? Sack her?

'That might be hours away. It's getting late, I'm shattered, and I haven't eaten yet.' And nor had he, she thought with a pang that she immediately chided herself for. Let the overbearing hypocrite starve.

After storming to the door, Konstantinos yanked it open. Immediately, a gust of snow streamed inside with a howl before he slammed the door back shut.

'You want to go out in that?' he demanded.

Having now seen, heard, and felt just how bad things were out there, Lena blanched at the thought of ski-walking through such torrid conditions.

Maybe he had a point after all.

'Okay, you're right, it doesn't look like we're going anywhere soon,' she said with fake brightness, casting her gaze anywhere but at him as she sought a solution. Thinking aloud, she said, 'I guess we'll just have to stay here for the night. There's an ice room free—you can have that. I'm sure you'll enjoy the experience. I'll take the store room.'

'You are not sleeping in the store room,' he said flatly. 'How many ice rooms are free?'

'Only the one and I'm not sleeping in it.'

'You are not sleeping on a floor, Lena.'

'We've got loads of sleeping bags. I'll make a nest for myself. I'll be fine. Or… I know. I can sleep on a sofa in the lounge.' The Igloo had a number of permanent heated facilities reached via a network of ice tunnels.

'Do I have to remind you that you're pregnant?'

Ignoring the thump of Rachel's jaw dropping to the floor, Lena rounded on him. 'No, you don't, but there is no way I am sleeping in one of those ice rooms, not after the last time.'

'Keep a light on if you're worried about the dark.'

'I thought you were worried about me endangering the baby?'

'A pregnant woman checked in this morning. We know there is no risk to the baby, not if you keep warm.'

'It's not keeping warm that worries me! Do you have any idea how terrifying a panic attack is when you're on your own?'

A pulse throbbed on the side of his jaw. 'You never mentioned a panic attack before.'

'I saw your reaction to my confession of claustrophobia. That was enough. I am not sleeping in an ice room and you have no right to try and bully me into it when we both know you hate the cold so much you'd sooner eat a ready meal than spend the night in one yourself.'

'I'll sleep in one with you if it stops you from sleeping on a floor or on a sofa.'

Totally taken aback, she stared at him.

He folded his arms across his chest and glowered at her. 'No pregnant woman should sleep on a floor or a sofa let alone the mother of my child. This is the only solution.'

'But...' Konstantinos's offer was so unexpected that for a moment she couldn't even think of a but. 'You *hate* the cold.'

'It is a sacrifice I am willing to make for our baby's sake,' Konstantinos said, knowing even as he said it that this wasn't quite the truth. It was the thought of Lena lying uncomfortably, trying to sleep on a hard floor after another long day that made his stomach twist and his chest clench, reactions only slightly less acute than when he'd thought he'd have to tie her to a chair to stop her going out into the treacherous blizzard. If she had gone, it would have been to spite him, he was certain of it.

Why had he goaded her like he'd done? Sure, he'd been angry with her for endangering herself and the baby by setting out in a blizzard...okay, he accepted Lena had set out when the conditions were better than they were now, and she was right that these conditions were perfectly normal to her and yes, there was the possibility he might have overreacted slightly to the situation…

A great sigh ripped its way through him.

It was his behaviour that had been faulty. Not Lena's. He'd commandeered a snowmobile he'd never driven before and set off in a blizzard in terrain that was alien to him. The fury that had driven him…it had not been normal anger. Not normal as he knew it. Fear had laced it. Fear for Lena.

He'd goaded her deliberately as punishment for frightening him. And to get a reaction.

Just as she'd understood the warning he'd given by relating Theo and Cassia's betrayal, now he understood where the bad temper he'd been carrying the entire day had come from. Lena had reacted to his warning in the exact way he'd hoped, by smothering any emotions so well they might well have been extinguished in their entirety, not even a glow in her eyes to hint at anything happening beneath her skin, nothing to indicate that the awareness that lay so heavily inside him for her was reciprocated; but instead of basking in relief that they could plan a cordial life as co-parents, he'd hated it. Hated the mask of calm serenity and professional politeness she wore around him.

What was it about this woman that provoked so many contradictory feelings in him? Why, seeing the stark abundance of emotions now shining in eyes that had been shuttered from him, did he feel like he wanted to fight through the blizzard to reach the moon and hand it to her as a gift?

A cough cut through the thickening silence.

They both blinked and turned their heads in unison.

Rachel was looking at them awkwardly. 'Shall I tell the staff we have extra guests for the night?'

Konstantinos turned back to Lena at the same moment she turned her stare back to him. Her shoulders rose slowly, colour heightening her cheeks before she gave a quick nod.

A surge of adrenaline he had no control over shot through him, making his heart pound and his pulse soar.

# CHAPTER NINE

LENA HAD TO force the steak she'd ordered from the Ice Restaurant down her throat. Being a heated permanent structure with soft lighting and cosy booths, the twenty-four-hour restaurant wasn't strictly part of The Igloo; instead, it connected to it in the same way its reception and lounge did, via the ice tunnel network. This was handy in bad weather such as they were currently experiencing, allowing guests and staff to use the permanent facilities without having to step outside. Most found the experience of staying in The Igloo exhilarating. They'd paid a fortune to sleep in an arthouse freezer and were determined to get their money's worth. Lena had found it terrifying.

This time, though, she wasn't frightened because of the fear of claustrophobia crawling its way back through her but because she would be sharing a bed with Konstantinos. Her only saving grace was that it could not be construed in any way as romantic. The cold meant they would both be fully clothed and in separate sleeping bags. In reality, it would be more like a childhood sleepover. Those reasonings did nothing to stop the food she'd managed to eat from churning in her stomach.

It didn't help that they were practically cut off from the other diners in the cosy, private booth or that she was so painfully aware of Konstantinos's foot resting so close to hers beneath the table or that she couldn't think of a single thing to say. There were so many emotions zooming through her that her brain couldn't cope with speech, too. Their entire meal had been conducted in excruciatingly tense silence, the excited blizzard chatter of those dining around them only making the silence between them more profound.

It was while they were eating their desserts that an alert came through on Lena's phone: the local airport would remain closed until at least 6 a.m.

Without speaking, she passed her phone to Konstantinos so he could see the alert for himself. He read it expressionlessly before meeting her stare. Jaw clenching, his shoulders rose and his nostrils flared before he gave a tight smile that clearly said, 'so be it.'

What didn't need to be said, verbally or otherwise, was that any vestige of hope that the blizzard would die out sooner rather than later had been dispelled. There would be no returning to their individual cabins tonight.

All too quickly, the point was reached where they could drag it out no longer. They were the last people in the restaurant. Their dessert plates were empty,

Konstantinos's second coffee and Lena's second hot chocolate had been drunk.

Even as she was thinking this, she still jumped when Konstantinos got abruptly to his feet. 'Come on. Let's do it.'

Taking a deep breath, she rose, too.

In silence they walked to the permanent heated changing rooms. Each ice room had its own designated changing room with a private bathroom and a locker to store possessions. Nothing could be taken into the ice room apart from the clothes on their backs. One of the American party from yesterday had ignored this instruction and been surprised to find his phone frozen solid to the ice bedside table he'd left it on overnight.

They stepped into their designated changing room. Their sleeping bags, pillows and a bag of toiletries had been placed on the bench that ran its short length. She felt Konstantinos's eyes dart to her and knew he'd picked up on the fact the sleeping bags they'd been given could be turned into a double, and it suddenly hit her fully that she would be spending the night sleeping beside the man she'd spent the past days desperately trying to turn her emotions away from and mentally dousing the awareness that vibrated through her just to look at him.

Those vibrations of awareness had ramped up during their excruciating meal and now, stuck within the tiny dimensions of the changing room, reached supersonic proportions.

Snatching up the bag of hotel-supplied toiletries,

she backed quickly to the bathroom. She didn't care if he wanted to use it first. She had to get away from him and get her head together, even if only for a few minutes. 'You need to take your layers off,' she said, the first words she'd spoken since they'd ordered their desserts. 'It's best just to sleep in your thermals and socks. Oh, and a hat. Bring your gloves and scarf, too, just in case.'

'We are sleeping in a freezer,' Konstantinos pointed out, wondering if she'd just spent the past couple of hours dreaming up the best way to get revenge on him being an arse to her.

'The sleeping bags are designed to withstand temperatures of up to minus forty.' Her speech was rapid, her hand gripped tightly to the handle of the bathroom door. 'Honestly, it's easier for your body to regulate itself this way. You'll need to wear your snowsuit and boots to the room but put everything else in the locker…except your jumper. Lots of people swear by putting that in the foot of your sleeping bag so you've something warm to put on in the morning before you have to get out of your cocoon or if you do get too cold during the night.'

She disappeared into the bathroom.

Alone, Konstantinos blew out air that would likely be one of his last warm breaths of the night, clenched his hands into fists, and rolled his neck and shoulders.

It was only one night and all they were sharing was a mattress, he reminded himself. After three nights of terrible, broken sleep, he was due a good one. The odds were he would fall asleep in minutes and when he woke, the blizzard would be over and so would the night. It would pass in a blink.

But even as he stripped his layers off as Lena had suggested—*was* she trying to induce hypothermia in him?—and repeated his mental pep talk, his thrumming body took delight in contradicting his thoughts, and when the handle of the bathroom turned ten minutes after she'd disappeared into it, the thick, heavy beats of his heart rippled.

She emerged smelling distinctly of toothpaste. Her gaze barely glanced him. She still wore her snowsuit but carried a neatly folded bundle of clothing, which she stashed in the locker. Maybe she wasn't trying to instigate hypothermia in him after all.

Once he'd finished in the bathroom and locked away anything that could freeze, Konstantinos gathered their sleeping bags and pillows and together they navigated the frozen tunnels decorated with tiny spheres of ice suspended from the ceiling to their designated room. The silence between them that had once again turned into a living entity was broken by Christmas carols playing out through cleverly concealed speakers and raucous voices and bursts of laughter that rang out as they neared the ice bar. Another tunnel and the door with their number on it greeted them.

The brightly lit ice vault they entered had clearly been inspired by Japanese culture. The perfectly curved walls were intricately carved into an arcade of cascading cherry blossom leading to a temple carved into the wall at the far end behind the king-sized ice bed, the mattress of which had already been laid with a thick insulating under-sheet and reindeer hides.

When the door closed, the silence was exactly as Lena had described it. Absolute. In an instant the frozen room shrank.

She pressed a switch by the door. The lights coming from the overhanging ice cherry blossom extinguished, leaving only the dim blue lights at the base of the tree trunks as faint illumination.

He looked at her sharply. 'Not too dark for you?'

She huddled her arms around herself, her gaze darting everywhere but at him as she shook her head. 'Neither of us will get any sleep if we keep the main light on.' Her voice barely rose above a whisper.

'If it gets too much, you tell me,' he ordered roughly; rough because he'd looked again at the bed and his insides had lurched and then bloomed like the carved blossom surrounding them to know that shortly they would lie side by side on it. 'Okay?'

He had to strain his ears to hear her whispered, 'Okay.'

He sucked in a frigid breath and decided to take the sticking plaster approach, stepping to the bed and laying the sleeping bags and pillows out. His heart thumped so hard his ribs were in danger of bruising.

Turning her back on him, she unzipped her snowsuit, then sat on the bed to remove her boots.

Konstantinos did the same, doing his best to tune out Lena's snowsuit sliding down her legs and off her feet, those same feet quickly slipping back into the boots, keeping his gaze averted when she hurried to the door to hang the snowsuit on a peg. Unfortunately, he wasn't quick enough to stop his eyes from darting to her when she hurried back to the bed. This time his heart thumped so hard he wouldn't have been surprised if it burst from his rib cage entirely.

She was rubbing her arms against the icy air. There was nothing sexy at all about what she was wearing. The cream thermal top and bottoms she wore covered her from neck to sock-covered foot. Under the blue glow of the barely there lights, though, her silhouette could have been sculpted from the same ice encasing them, and suddenly a memory flashed in his mind of when that same silhouette— with one obvious difference—had taken his breath away without any warning.

When Thom had recommended Lena as his replacement, Konstantinos had struggled to picture whom he was talking about. He employed thousands of staff worldwide. It was impossible to know each individual face. He went through the staff files to put a face to Lena's name and was surprised to discover that yes, she must have made an impression on some base level as he did vaguely recognise her, but then thought no more about it. A week later he'd flown in to conduct the interviews.

When Lena had entered the meeting room for her interview, the clouds that had been hiding the sun suddenly parted. Its rays had shone through the window and landed straight on her. Whatever trickery had taken place, for one brief moment his mind had interpreted Lena's silhouette as being cast in gold.

But it was when she'd smiled at him that his breath had been truly stolen, he now remembered, remembering, too, the way his blood had pumped when she'd slid into the chair across from his. Of course, he'd gotten those strange bodily happenings under firm control. So firm that he'd cast them from his memory. Cast from it, too, how his interview with Lena had gone on for three times as long as all the other interviews for no discernible reason whatsoever, and the extra special care he'd taken when shaving before their celebratory meal, and the strange way he'd reacted when he'd seen her for the first time dressed in something other than her staff uniform. The red blouse she'd worn and tight black trousers had not been in the least revealing but, *Theos*, they had made his blood pump hard.

All that had happened before they'd shared three bottles of wine and his subconscious had finally forced to the forefront of his mind that Lena Weir was the most beautiful woman he'd ever set eyes on.

How had he forgotten all that?

And now he had to fight to draw breath, unable to drag his stare away from the feminine beauty coming towards him. The generous swell of her unbound breasts jutted...he almost groaned as the memory of their taste danced on his tongue...beneath the fabric, hips gently swaying... And then her boots were off and she was on the bed and quickly lining her sleeping bag with the insulating sheet they'd each been provided with and sliding her legs into it, reaching for the zip at the bottom and—

Her eyes suddenly locked on to his.

A pulse of desire shot through him, so strong it stole whatever breath he had left.

Even under the dim lighting he could see the colour crawl over her cheeks, see the way her lips pulled in together before she whispered with a shiver, 'You're going to freeze if you don't get into your sleeping bag.'

Freeze? Even with the cloud of vapour that came with the exhale of the breath he'd finally managed to make, the last thing he felt right then was cold. One look at his groin and Lena would see for herself the heat of his arousal for her.

Somehow, he managed to pull himself upright and carry his snowsuit to hang beside hers.

When he turned back to face her, she was co-cooned in her sleeping bag, only her cute nose and cheeks showing through.

Lena knew it was dangerous to peek at Konstan-tinos as his long legs carried him back to the bed, especially after she'd just caught him staring at her with that glint in his eyes that shot straight into her pelvis, but she was helpless to resist. One look was too much and she squeezed them tightly shut and quickly rolled over so her back would be to him, and tried desperately hard to get air into her lungs.

How could just looking at him cause such inter-nal devastation? How could she explain the pain-ful wrench of her heart and the aching throbs deep between her legs just to catch a glimpse of the soft black hair poking out at the neck of the black thermal top he wore?

The mattress dipped. She held her breath, squeezed her eyes even tighter, and gripped even harder to her biceps. She didn't know if she was holding herself so tightly because of the cold or as protection against him... No, she realised painfully, it was protection against herself. She would not act the role of hopeless, lust-riddled adolescent again.

Once he'd made himself comfortable, the silence in the room was complete. The only sounds Lena could hear clearly were the rapid beats of her heart and the short intakes of breath she managed to snatch.

She cocooned herself closer into her sleeping bag and wished she'd remembered to put her scarf on. She'd been in such a flux in the changing room that she'd thoughtlessly added it to the pile of layers she'd stuck in the locker. After her babbled words of advice to Konstantinos, she'd stupidly forgotten to bring a jumper, too. Her nose was cold.

Time passed. Not a single sound or movement came from the body lying beside her. She remembered waking between making love on their night together and watching him sleep through the light that still managed to filter in through the blackout blinds. She'd been fascinated. Her dad's snoring was so loud he was capable of waking the whole street up but Konstantinos slept without sound, only the deep rise and fall of his chest proving he was actually alive.

The urge to roll over and press herself as close as their individual sleeping bags would allow was unbearable.

Her brain wouldn't switch off. Her thoughts were spinning like a carousel. She could no longer keep her eyes closed. She wished desperately for Konstantinos to wake up and say something, anything to break the silence closing in on her. The longer the minutes ticked by, the more images of the past flickered in her vision, and the more the impenetrable dark shadowed walls closed in on her, and the deeper the muffled effect of the solid block of ice and snow they were encased in. The beats of her already erratic heart changed to a frighteningly ragged tempo, snatches of breath becoming almost impossible to find.

Despite his best efforts to relax his body so sleep would take him into oblivion, Konstantinos's best efforts were nowhere near good enough. He was aiming for the impossible. He was just too intensely aware of Lena huddled on the other side of the bed to relax, his senses attuned to her every breath and every tiny body adjustment. It was only now that he was lying within this ice vault that he truly understood what she meant about the silence being a silence like no other. Nothing penetrated the thick walls. It was just the two of them cocooned away from the world. Him and Lena.

It was the sharp gasping turn her breaths took that

first alerted him to there being something wrong. If he was a dog his ears would have pricked up. He didn't need to be any animal other than human to sense the new form the tension that had laced her since she'd accepted they would have to share a bed for the night took.

And then came the faint hum of strained vocal cords. If they were anywhere but here, he wouldn't have heard it.

'Lena?' Alarmed, he rolled over. 'Are you okay?'

She didn't answer, just repeated the tune, but this time more clearly, enabling him to define the words of a song that made no sense at all. 'The big ship sails on the Alley Alley O...' A swallow. 'The Alley Alley O, the Alley Alley O.' Another swallow. 'The big ship sails on the Alley Alley O, on the last day of September.'

Instinct made him unzip his sleeping bag enough to free his arms so he could wrap them around her and spoon himself around her. She didn't resist. A hand poked out of the top of her sleeping bag and clawed for his. He caught it and held it tightly, pressing himself closer to her; all the while she sang another refrain of the strange childlike verse.

'Better?' he asked when the singing finally petered away.

When her answer came, it was a choked, 'Thank you.'

He squeezed her hand. She squeezed back.

'Is it always like that?' he asked quietly.

Lena shook her head. She hadn't had a panic at-

tack since the last time she'd slept in The Igloo. That
time she'd managed to slam the switch installed at
the side of the bed and get some light into the room
but the attack had continued for another fifteen minutes. This time its grip on her had lessened the moment Konstantinos spoke her name. The effect of his
arms being wrapped around her and the clasp of his
strong, comforting hand had soothed her more ef-
fectively than even her mother had been able to do
when the panic attacks were at their height.

'Thank you,' she repeated. His arms tightened, his
forehead pressing into the hood of her sleeping bag.

Lena's heart throbbed and tears filled her eyes.
That Konstantinos was putting himself through what
was for him personal torture just so she didn't have
to sleep alone in her own version of it meant more
than she could ever say. She wished she hadn't been
so angry with his hypocritical sanctimony and then
too full of fear that sharing a bed would see her betray her deep yearning for him to recognise it earlier.
Having his arms around her and the strength of his
body tight against her made her feel like a woman
drowning in an ocean storm lifted onto a life boat
and gently steered into calm waters.

'You must be cold,' she whispered once she'd kept
the tears at bay. He'd disentangled himself from his
warm cocoon to comfort her, and now her panic had
subsided, other, far more dangerous, feelings were
creeping through her, the beats of her heart thumping with that weighted raggedy sensation.

'It's okay,' he said, as if potential hypothermia

was nothing, and suddenly she was filled with another emotion so powerful it knocked the breath out of her. Konstantinos had put his health at risk for her.

Overtaken by the need to look at him, she shifted just enough to roll onto her back without losing the solid strength of his lean body compressed against her and without releasing his hand. 'It's not okay. You'll get frostbite or something.'

He lifted his head. The dim blue lighting kept so much of his vampiric features hidden in shadows, but what she found in his hooded gaze made her pelvis throb and her heart swell so hard and so fast it crushed her lungs.

Unthinkingly, she let go of his hand and placed her fingers on his smooth neck. The shock of cold she found there melted her insides that little bit more. His skin was cold for her. Because he'd comforted her when she'd needed him. She swallowed hard. She didn't want to let him go. She wanted him to crawl into her sleeping bag and share the warmth his care had filled her with. 'Tinos, you're freezing.'

Konstantinos's heart clenched at the shortening of his name, the clench twisting painfully to see what was shining in Lena's eyes and know it was what she must be seeing in his own eyes.

He tried to draw in air.

Who was he trying to fool? The more he tried to fight this combustible mix of emotions and desire that burned in his veins for Lena, the worse it got. The deeper it infected him. The more he wanted her. Wanted her like he'd never wanted anyone or anything.

Did he seriously think he could live his life with Lena Weir in it without waging a constant battle with himself?

Palming her cheek, he stared at her beautiful face, wondering how someone Aphrodite would envy could look at him and not be repulsed. Look at him with desire... No, more than desire. Like he meant something to her. Just as he was coming to see that she meant something to him...

Slowly, he brought his mouth down to hers.

# CHAPTER TEN

THE TENDER MELDING of Konstantinos's lips against hers melted the last of the defences Lena had tried so hard to protect herself with.

There was nothing of the hard, scorched fury of the passionate kiss they'd shared in her cabin the other night but the emotion she could feel contained in it made her heart beat twice as hard and as fast.

He lifted his head again. His smile was crooked. 'Your nose is cold,' he said hoarsely, before pressing a kiss to the tip and sitting up. Working quickly, he unzipped the rest of his sleeping bag, then lay on his side to unzip Lena's. There was a shock of cold on the side of her body exposed to the frozen air but no time for it to properly penetrate her skin for Konstantinos immediately used his own body as cover to protect her from the chill, and got to work on opening their individual liners and zipping the two sleeping bags together.

By the time they were secured together tightly, he was shivering. When he groped for her hands, it was like being touched by blocks of ice.

'Burrow under,' she whispered urgently, pulling his hands together and holding them against her belly while rubbing them with her own, then wriggling down as low as she could in their newly created cocoon. As soon as he'd followed suit, his knees bent as much as the tightness of the conjoined sleeping bags would allow to accommodate his tall frame, she abandoned his hands and hooked her thigh over his hip, burrowed her face into his neck and breathed into his skin, wrapping her arms tightly around his waist and vigorously stroking his back, pressing every inch of herself that she could into him, doing everything she could to replace the warmth he'd lost for her.

The single-minded determination and care Lena was displaying as she used her whole body to bring warmth back into him touched Konstantinos immeasurably. His wealth and status meant people often tripped over themselves to ensure his every need was taken care of, but it was never out of concern for him as a man. Those people never saw him as anything but a billionaire with the power and contacts to be their meal ticket if they played their cards right. His lovers viewed him through the prism of his fat wallet. He couldn't even imagine Cassia in the long-ago days when she'd proclaimed to love him doing anything but lie there with the expectation that he do all the work needed to keep them warm.

Lena was having his child. She would spend the rest of her life without a single financial worry and she knew it. He was no potential meal ticket for her:

the ticket had already been cashed. And yet, despite all this, despite there being no benefit to herself, she was trying her hardest to fight the cold for him.

Every stroke of her small hands over his back and shoulders and arms, every rub of her thighs and calves over his legs and hips, every hot breath blown onto his neck and jaw, spoke louder than words that he did mean something to her. A part of her genuinely cared for him. For *him*.

He didn't know if it was her tender ministrations or this astounding realisation that filled his chest with the final dose of heat needed to shake off the last of the chills, but it was Lena who'd filled it, and he roamed his hands over her body in turn, revelling in the softness of her contours through the clothing she wore, marvelling at the subtle changes to it since their night together, marvelling that he remembered every part of their night together so well that he could actually feel the changes pregnancy had made. Those changes only fed the desire that constantly burned for her. Clasping her peachy bottom, he rolled her onto her back, taking care not to squash her with his weight. Dim light poured through the opening his movements had created at the top of their tight nest, and he stared down at her in wonder.

Her hand moved to palm the back of his neck. It burned at her touch. 'That's better,' she whispered.

He had to swallow the lump that had formed in his throat. His face was barely inches above hers. 'Are you warm enough?'

Their private cocoon muffled their words, adding to the sensation that it was only the two of them in this whole wide world.

She smiled tremulously and razed her fingers through the hair at his nape. 'I am now.' And then she raised her face and kissed him.

Lena closed her eyes and sank into the slow, gentle fusion of their mouths. Her already overloaded senses greedily soaked in all the new sensations filling them, from Konstantinos's dark taste as the kiss deepened and he parted her lips with a push of his tongue, to the scratching of his stubble against her skin.

Something had shifted between them that night. And something had shifted in her, too. It had started when he'd held her so protectively during her panic attack and grown when she'd smothered his body to warm him, the awakening of a deep, primitive need to protect him just as he'd protected her.

And she knew he felt it, too. Whether the wall Konstantinos had built around himself to insulate him from pain in the wake of his brother and fiancée's betrayal was falling down because of the baby didn't matter. He was opening himself to *her*. It was there in his voice, in his every touch, and she responded to it like a moth to a flame. She was the moth and she'd carried his flame since the night they'd conceived their child.

With the tight enclosure they were trapped within preventing them from ripping off the barrier of their clothing, Lena could do nothing but hold him closely, wind her legs around his waist and drink in the ever-deepening kisses that sent sensation thrumming through her entire being and enveloped her in a cloud that contained only him.

How she'd adored touching him that night, exploring Konstantinos in a way she'd never done before; had never *wanted* to do before. And how she'd ached for *his* touch, a desperation to have his mouth and hands on every inch of her skin, opening herself to him in a way she'd never dreamed she was capable of. That burn was alive in her again, a burn to peel their layers off and get as physically close as it was possible to be, but as that was impossible, she would make the most of what they could share because right now this was as close to heaven as her delirious body was able to get.

Deeper still their kisses forged, an utter devouring of mouths and tongues, an assault of hands and fingers scraping and groping every inch of the other they could reach within the tight, tight confines. The weight of Konstantinos's arousal pressed tantalisingly against her flaming pelvis, sending such thrills through her that she could have wept for his possession.

'*Theos*, Lena, I want you so much,' he groaned into her mouth as he ground his erection against her, making her moan.

She clasped the back of his head and kissed him with all the passion she possessed and pressed her pelvis tighter against him, showing him with her body how badly she needed him. The burn inside her was fast turning into molten agony. 'Please,' she begged. 'Please.'

The beats of Konstantinos's heart had never pumped so hard. His blood had never felt so thick. Arousal had never felt like pain.

He didn't just want Lena. He needed her. Needed to be inside her, however impossible it seemed at that moment, because in that moment it felt as necessary as breathing.

The confinement of their wrappings against the freezing temperatures left little room for movement but enough for him to grip the waistband of her leggings. She lifted her bottom enough for him to yank them down to her thighs and then helped him yank his own past his hips, freeing his arousal to press heavily against the heat it so desperately needed to take possession of. The nails of one hand scratching into his hair, she grabbed his buttock with the other and writhed against him, her unashamed desire coming close to blowing his mind. It had been like that during their night together, a rabid hunger that had consumed them both.

*Theos*, he was trembling. She was trembling.

Aching to be inside her but with Lena's bunched clothing preventing their bodies from locking together in the way they both so desperately needed, he had to hold his erection and, with her plaintive urgings, guide himself into the slick heat. It was impossible to thrust the whole of himself inside her but it didn't matter. If this was all they could have then he would take it. All that mattered was this electrifying fusion of their bodies that zinged into his entire being.

'Oh, God,' she whispered breathlessly, her teeth razing over his cheek. 'Please, Tinos. Please.'

Sliding a hand behind her bottom, he gripped it tightly and began to move.

Tongues entwined, they found a slow rhythm that managed to give them both what they needed, their passionate kisses punctuated by gasps and moans of pleasure.

Lena was lost in a world of sensation. Lost in a world of Konstantinos and the slowly increasing pressure coiling so tightly inside her that came only from him. Only from him.

She was his, she thought dimly as the pressure built into a peak that exploded and had her crying out his name, sending her soaring on a kaleidoscope of sensation so intense the colours swirled together and white lights flickered behind her eyes.

This was like nothing Konstantinos had ever experienced. He didn't care that he couldn't be buried as deep inside Lena as it was possible to be; what they were sharing was beyond comprehension. And so he didn't try to understand, just closed his thoughts off to everything but Lena, her scent, the taste of her mouth, and the exquisite pleasure of their bodies crushed together until his name spilled from her lips as a cry and her climax pulled him over the edge and into the abyss.

\* \* \*

Lena's eyes fluttered open. The sleeping bag covered so much of her face that she was struggling to breathe. The darkness was as all encompassing as it had been before she'd drifted into that excuse for sleep but, other than the bit of her forehead exposed between where her hat rested on it and the sleeping bag started, she was as warm as she'd ever been. Cosily warm. How could she be anything else when she had Konstantinos pressed so snugly against her back and his arms wrapped around her?

She had no idea what the time was but instinct told her twilight—not that it existed here at this time of year—had long passed.

Reluctantly letting go of his arm, she pinched the top of the sleeping bag covering her mouth and nose, drew it down to her chin and inhaled the frigid air into her lungs.

His arms tightened around her. 'Are you okay?'

Konstantinos's sleepy voice made her chest expand. Putting her hand back on his arm, she gently squeezed. 'I'm fine. Go back to sleep.'

He shifted his head to rest his chin on her shoulder. 'You sure? If you have another panic attack coming, tell me. Let me help you.'

Oh, she could choke from the emotions filling her. 'Not another attack, I promise. I just needed air.'

He kissed her neck and slipped a hand beneath her top.

She groped for it, threading her fingers through

his, and closed her eyes at the simple pleasure of his flesh against hers.

This was the most dangerous time. She knew it. She'd woken in the witching hours the night they'd conceived their child feeling like she'd woken in heaven, Konstantinos's hot mouth already urgent against hers, his possession of her almost savage in its intensity. She'd never have believed in those blissful moments that a few hours later he would look her in the eye and tell her it had been a mistake. She wanted desperately to believe that this time it would be different, that having a baby together made it different, but how could she trust that, especially with the warnings he'd given her barely forty-eight hours ago? What had happened that night hadn't been planned. A spell had been cast over them and she was terrified that when the bright lights that indicated daytime were switched on, the spell would be broken for him, just as it had been the last time.

'How long have you suffered with them?' he asked quietly, his chin still resting on her shoulder.

'I don't really suffer them anymore.'

'Then what was it you suffered earlier?' he asked in a dry, indulgent tone that made her smile and wish so hard for things she shouldn't wish for.

'It was my first one in four years.'

'So the last one was when you stayed the night in The Igloo for the first time?'

'Yes. I wouldn't have applied to work here if the attacks weren't under control. I didn't know I'd become claustrophobic. If I had, I wouldn't have stayed in The Igloo and the panic attack wouldn't have happened.'

'If you had them under control does that mean there was a time when they were out of control?'

Lena thought back to the time when having up to ten panic attacks a day was considered normal. Terrifying but normal. 'I don't know about out of control but they were pretty frequent.'

'Is it something you always suffered with?'

'No.'

'So when did they start?'

'Six years ago.'

'So around the time your sister had her accident?'

'Yes.'

If Konstantinos squeezed her any tighter he feared crushing her bones. He didn't understand why he felt the need to hold Lena so closely to him but, for that night, he accepted that whatever they were sharing was a spell of its own making.

With her hand resting on top of his, he made smooth circular motions over her belly. Earlier, after they'd straightened themselves up as best they could and he'd wrapped her into his arms, he'd put his hand to her belly like he was doing now and felt their baby move beneath his palm. He'd drifted off to sleep filled with emotions deep enough to choke him. 'What happened?'

She sighed and twisted in his arms so she lay on

her back, and palmed his cheek. 'I was in the car with her.'

Ice spooled in his veins. 'When the accident happened?'

'Yes. It was my nineteenth birthday. We'd gone out with friends. Heidi wasn't a big drinker and offered to drive. We were driving back home when we were hit side-on by a drunk driver. We ended up upside down in a ditch.'

Konstantinos was glad she was no longer spooned against him or he feared he really would have crushed her bones at that.

Spreading his palm flat, he slid it round her back and pressed his mouth to her forehead. 'What injuries did you suffer?'

'Nothing serious. The other car hit the driver's door. Heidi was... I thought...'

'What?' he encouraged gently, his chest filling with the ice crawling through his veins to guess what she struggled to say.

'I thought she was dead.' Lena blew out a choked puff of air and fought back tears as the terror she'd experienced when she'd begged and begged her unresponsive sister to wake up came back to her in full technicolour. 'I was so scared, Tinos. I couldn't get to my phone to call for help. It was pitch-black but I could smell blood and I knew it wasn't coming from me but from her, and I couldn't release my seat belt and get to my phone. I was hanging upside down and so disoriented and Heidi was upside down, too, like something out of a horror film, and she wasn't answering me and I could smell her blood and there was nothing I could do...and...'

Dimly aware she was on the verge of talking herself into another panic attack, Lena closed her eyes and moved her face closer to Konstantinos's neck so she could inhale his comforting scent. 'The big ship sails on the Alley Alley O,' she sang to herself, a technique her mother had read about and which, with the therapist's encouragement, had become the tool Lena had developed to control the attacks. 'On the last day of September.'

'How long were you there?' he asked into the silence.

She breathed in his musky scent again before answering. 'Only ten minutes or so—the accident was witnessed. But they were the longest minutes of my entire life. It felt like hours. The couple who witnessed it found us but by that stage I'd convinced myself I was going to die there, too, but I walked out of the hospital without a scratch on me.'

'Not physical scratches,' he murmured before kissing her forehead. 'But you were scarred in other ways.'

'Those scars are nothing. I'm healthy. I can walk. I can do everything for myself. I can feed myself and bathe myself. I can breathe unaided. I'm not prone to infections. I can have children. Heidi will never have any of that, and it makes me want to cry because she's the one who was always maternal, not me. When we were kids we played mummies and daddies and I always played the role of daddy because she insisted on being mummy. She always knew she wanted to marry and have a family whereas I was always indifferent. Children weren't even on my radar. Every hope and dream she ever had is dead and still she smiles and keeps cheerful and makes the best of each day, and she insists that I do, too. Remember you asked why I was here and not at home supporting my family?'

He gave a pained sigh. 'Lena, I am sorry. I should never have said that.'

'Believe me, it's nothing I haven't thought a thousand times. Why should I get to live my dream when Heidi lost *everything*? But she wanted me to go. Even when the panic attacks were still coming thick and fast she'd nag at me to go.'

'And your parents?'

'They wanted me to go, too. The three of them ganged up on me, the line of attack being that as Heidi had lost her health and her dreams, it was only right that I make the most of mine. It was Dad who spotted the advert for a receptionist here—he took it on himself to subscribe to a load of Swedish recruitment websites. Sweden was always my favourite place. I lived for the summers and Christmases we spent here. It was always my dream to live out here in the snow and ride huskies. He made me apply. They all did. They even had a leaving party for me. If Heidi could have jumped out of her wheelchair and helped me pack my suitcase, she would have done.'

'But you still feel guilt,' he guessed.

She took a long time to answer. 'It's always there. I can never shake it that while I'm living a full life, she's confined to a wheelchair and completely dependent.'

'Is that the real reason you haven't told your family about the baby? Are you afraid your news will hurt her?'

'I don't...' She swallowed. 'I hadn't thought of it like that. Maybe that's played a part in it.'

Remembering his trawl through the Ice Hotel staff's social media accounts and how Lena was mostly absent from the socialising that played such a big part in their off-the-clock lives, Konstantinos would guess it had played more than a part. He could understand her position as general manager would make her feel the need to remain above the wilder behaviour that sometimes gripped them, but she'd only had the role for five months. There was no indication she'd ever joined in the socialising in the way it was embraced by everyone else.

He'd trawled through those accounts seeking evidence that another man could be the father of her baby, he remembered with painful guilt.

'Tell me something else,' he said. 'Is Heidi the reason I'm your first lover since the accident? Am I wrong in assuming it was the accident that stopped you forming relationships?'

'I've only ever had one proper boyfriend,' she confessed. 'He ended it when he went off to uni a couple of months before the accident. Once the accident happened I didn't have the headspace to even think about relationships.'

'But you've been here for four years. You're beautiful. People are drawn to you. I can't imagine you've been single all this time by choice.'

'I've had offers for want of a better word but I was never interested.'

'Still pining for your first love?' For some reason he had to unlock his jaw to ask that.

'Lord, no.' For the first time since she'd started opening up to him, there was a lighter tone to her voice. 'James and I... I hate to admit this but I was really shallow in those days. The only thing I liked about him was his face. He was gorgeous. All the girls fancied him. I cried for a week after he ended it but really, that's because I was being dramatic. There was no real substance to my feelings for him. I just liked being seen with him.'

'If it's pretty faces you like, why end your celibacy with me?'

# CHAPTER ELEVEN

FOR SOMEONE WHO was half Konstantinos's size and five months pregnant, Lena twisted round and pushed him flat on his back with a surprising agility.

'Now, you listen to me, Konstantinos Siopis,' she said fiercely, speaking right in his face. 'You are *not* ugly, and to put you right from what you accused me of the other day, I didn't sleep with you because you're rich or, just in case you're thinking it, because you're my boss, or even because of the wine I'd drunk. I slept with you because I couldn't not. You smiled at me… I'd never seen you smile before…and I felt it right in the place our baby's now growing.'

He gazed into the eyes glaring vehemently at him and felt something move in his heart.

Her face still hovering over his, she palmed his stubbled cheek. 'I have never felt *anything* like that before. You're not handsome, Tinos, but to my eyes you're beautiful. Every bit of you.'

He attempted humour to lighten the weight building in his chest. 'Even my nose?'

She kissed the tip. 'Every bit of you.'

'My brother broke it when I was eleven. That's why it bends.'

Something flashed in her eyes. 'Why did he do that?'

'We were fighting and he hit me. In fairness, I hit him first. The damage only became pronounced in my teenage years.' At the age of fourteen he'd suddenly shot up, growing six inches in the same number of months. His face had changed, too, becoming angular, his always too-long nose gaining prominence. It had taken Theo and Cassia's betrayal for him to understand that outer beauty often masked inner ugliness. That was when he'd stopped caring about his appearance. People could take him or leave him, and as his wealth had grown, people, especially women, had increasingly taken him.

Right now, here with Lena, he felt like he was with the first person who'd ever looked beneath the surface to see *him*.

'What were you fighting about?' she asked.

'I can't remember. We were always fighting in those days.'

'Sibling rivalry at its finest. Heidi and I hardly ever fought but I had friends who hated their siblings. Who's the oldest?'

'He is, by two years.'

'Strange,' she mused. 'It's usually the younger sibling who tries to outshine the older one and take what they have for themselves. He must have been incredibly jealous of you.'

He grunted a laugh. 'He had nothing to be jealous

about. Theo's the one who had everything. He was movie-star handsome like your ex, and like your ex all the girls wanted him.' Those who'd befriended Konstantinos like Cassia had done so in the hope of getting closer to his brother. Even his parents had noticed the surge in young female applicants for the rare job vacancies in the family restaurant once Theo had started working there.

Her face tightened, that flash blazing in her eyes again. '*Exactly.* Tinos, he stole your fiancée. That's the cruellest thing a sibling can do. He stuck around to work in the family restaurant, didn't he?'

Fascinated at her obvious anger, he nodded.

The blaze continued to flash. 'I bet he hated your hard work and success taking the spotlight from him so he stole the one thing that meant something to you.'

'He fell in love with her.' Konstantinos was aware he was only defending his brother to provoke more of this reaction from Lena.

'I don't care. If he found himself developing feelings for her he should have stayed the hell away.'

Gazing into the face of the woman *he* should have stayed the hell away from, Konstantinos asked for the first time, not only aloud but to himself, 'What if he couldn't?'

Hadn't he been unable to keep away from Lena? For all the excuses he'd made, hadn't he flown back to Sweden seven months early because his craving to see her again had grown too strong to resist any longer?

'Oh, come on,' she said, oblivious to his new direction of thought. 'He was an adult, not an adolescent experiencing hormones for the first time. There is no excuse for what he did to you. None. They deserve each other and I hope their marriage is a living hell for them both.'

With amusement building amidst the weight in his chest, he slipped his hand back under her top. *Theos*, he loved Lena's skin, the soft texture, the way she shivered with obvious pleasure at his touch. Arousal spooled in his loins to imagine stripping her naked and making love to her with his hands and mouth, tasting every inch, licking the tips of her breasts in the way that had made her pant and plead and beg for more...

'I hate to disappoint you but my parents tell me they are happy,' he said, having to blink his concentration back to their conversation and not to the heady fantasies that had made him as stiff as a board.

'There's still time for karma to bite them on their butts,' she said stubbornly, even as she slipped her hand up his top and splayed her fingers through the hairs on his abdomen.

No one had ever taken his side without equivocation before. All these years, the ghost of Theo and Cassia had tainted every minute spent with his parents and extended family. He'd never expected anyone to take sides, least of all his parents, but expectation and want were two different things, and their love for their two sons and determination not to choose one over the other had festered like a wound.

Konstantinos had been wronged. His life had been shattered. His trust had been destroyed. His dreams had gone up in smoke. And no one had taken his part, making every excuse under the damned sun to excuse the golden son's betrayal.

'Where does this fire come from?' he wondered idly as he continued to gaze at her, his mouth filling with moisture to imagine those lips currently set in an obstinate, furious line kissing fire over his skin. That this fury was on his behalf...

Her shadowed brow creased. 'I just think they treated you abysmally.'

*Theos*, she was beautiful.

Cupping her head, he pulled her down and kissed her, delighting when her obstinate lips sighed into his and returned the kiss with the same hunger consuming him.

With a soft moan into his mouth, she stretched her body half over his and slipped a thigh between his legs.

Twelve hours ago Konstantinos would have said it impossible that he would spend a night in The Igloo and wish for the morning not to come. And when Lena's hand slipped down his abdomen, then lower still and took his arousal in her hand with a groan and made a fist around it that made *him* groan, he closed his eyes and wished even harder for this night to go on forever.

'I've never ridden with huskies,' Konstantinos said. They were still huddled in their cocoon, Lena's face resting on the top of his chest, his hands making circular strokes over her back, her fingers making circular strokes around his nipple.

'What, never?' she asked in mock horror. 'You've owned this place forever and first you tell me you've never seen the Northern Lights and now you tell me you've never been on a husky ride?'

'Explain what I'm missing out on being dragged through snow in freezing temperatures?'

'The exhilaration of it all! You're out in the wilderness, your eyes are streaming because of the freshness of the air as it whips through your face—'

'The freshness of the air because it's so cold?'

She laughed. 'That's all part of the fun of it.'

'I will take your word for that.'

'Try it for yourself. You might surprise yourself and find you enjoy it.'

He gave a disbelieving grunt. She pinched his nipple. Before he could react in the way her body was already thrumming with anticipation for, there was a knock on the door.

Lena's deliriously happy mood plummeted.

The knock indicated that their night in The Igloo was officially over.

The door opened. It was always that way. The acoustics of The Igloo made it as impossible for sound to travel out of the individual rooms as it was for it to travel in. The knock was nothing but a polite courtesy.

Johan, the member of staff going from room to room with hot drinks, had clearly been prepped for who to expect in this particular one as he didn't even flicker to find the owner of the hotel and its general manager sharing the bed, or raise a brow that they'd zipped their sleeping bags together.

'Good morning,' he said cheerfully. 'Hot lingon-berry juice?' A moment later the main lights were switched on.

So stark was the change in illumination that Lena had to wait for her eyes to adjust before she was able, working in tandem with Konstantinos, to sit upright.

Johan poured them both a mug of the steaming liquid and then carried their snowsuits over to them before leaving them to drink and get changed in privacy.

Cradling her mug in both hands, Lena found herself scared to look at Konstantinos even though their cocoon meant the sides of their bodies were still pressed tightly together.

With the knock of a door and the switch of a light, the spell had been broken.

Their whole night together, opening up to each other, making love, opening up even more, bringing each other to climax using only their hands, and then all the silly inconsequential chatter about everything and nothing that was neither silly nor inconsequential, the words an unceasing flow of reminiscences, potted histories, likes and dislikes with no question of wasting their precious time sleeping, and all that time holding each other, at one with each other, just them in the whole world...

And now it was over.

'What are you thinking?' he asked after the silence left in Johan's wake had grown to unbearable levels.

She swallowed and tried to keep the despondency from her voice. 'Nothing interesting.'

'Lena, look at me.'

If his order hadn't been so gently delivered, she would have ignored him.

What she found on his face made her heart throb.

Hooded eyes not leaving hers, he placed his empty mug beside him on the mattress and then rubbed his thumb along her cheekbone. 'That was no mistake,' he said quietly.

She tried to take in air. Afraid she would cry if she spoke, she bit her bottom lip.

His smile was crooked. It beamed straight into her swelling heart. 'Come back to my cabin with me.'

Now she wanted to wail like a child. 'I can't. I've got to work.'

'You need to sleep. Sven can cover for you—he'll be doing it for real in a few days. If need be, he can make any rearrangements to the rota.' Straightening her hat for her, he kissed the tip of her nose.

After a night spent in such confinement, the sheer size of Konstantinos's cabin was a stark relief to Lena. She rarely needed to enter the guest cabins and the last time she'd been in here, things had been so fraught between them that she hadn't appreciated how luxurious and inviting it was. The bed at the far end, behind the proper living area and proper dining area, was so large and filled with such plump pillows she took one look at it and felt the exhaustion of a night without sleep hit her.

He smoothed her hair off her face and cradled her cheeks. 'Shower and sleep?'

She nodded. Lethargy had gripped her so tightly her tongue felt too thick to speak.

Taking her hand, he led her into the bathroom. She gazed with longing at the huge rolltop bath but he shook his head. 'You'll fall asleep in it. Another time.'

Another time. She liked the sound of that.

She liked even more when he stripped all his clothes off then helped her strip off, too, liked more than that when he stood under the spray of the walk-in shower with her, and liked even more than that when he massaged shower gel over every inch of her skin and lathered shampoo into her hair. By the time he was finished, she was so relaxed she could have fallen asleep on her feet. Once they were dry and their teeth brushed, he got a huge, dry, fluffy towel, wrapped it around her, lifted her into his arms and carried her to bed.

The last thing she felt as she slipped into oblivion was Konstantinos's arms wrapping around her.

'Come on,' Lena cajoled. 'It's our last night here.'

'I'm not going outside,' Konstantinos said firmly. 'It's freezing out there.'

'It's always freezing out there.'

'And I only go out in it when it's strictly necessary.'

She didn't argue with him. No, she did better than that. Lena simply folded her arms under her breasts and stared at him with that look he was coming to recognise. It was the same look she'd given when they'd argued over which house would be more suitable for her and their child. He'd wanted the one in a plush gated community. She'd wanted the one in the middle of nowhere. Both were a ten-minute drive from her parents' home town. Lena, he was coming to understand, loved the unpolluted night sky, which is what their latest standoff was about. The night sky--yes, he knew, it was currently always a night sky here—was cloudless, and Lena wanted them to leave the warmth of his cabin and stand in conditions colder than a freezer to look at it.

She'd won the standoff over the house, and, with a resigned sigh, he admitted defeat over getting frostbite. If he didn't know better he would think Lena had him eating out of her hands.

Climbing off the bed he'd been trying to entice her into joining him on so he could make love to her again, Konstantinos hooked an arm around her waist and pulled her to him. 'If I do this, you will owe me.'

Her amazing dark brown eyes gleamed. 'If you stay outside with me for more than an hour, I will owe you *big* time.'

Gripping her bottom so he could press his arousal against her, he murmured, 'Can I take part payment now?'

She rose onto her toes, a hand sliding down his naked abdomen to take his throbbing excitement into her hand. With a gentle squeeze, she whispered into his ear, 'Nope. A full hour, Mr Siopis, and then we can come back in here and I will strip naked for you and let you do whatever you want.'

He groaned, then groaned even louder when she dropped his erection and skipped out of his hold and well out of arm's reach. Her gaze drifted down to his jutting arousal and she gave a mischievous smile. 'The cold outside will cure that for you.'

Okay, Konstantinos thought an hour later, huddled on one of the hotel's viewing benches, a ten-minute trek away from the lights of the main complex, Lena might have a point about the beauty of the night sky here. The moonless vast sky was alight with stars, high above them a long streak of hazy light with a high concentration of what looked like cloud interspersed with thousands of massed stars which she authoritatively told him was the Milky Way, explaining how Earth was located on one of its spiral arms and that was what enabled them to see its centre so clearly.

'See?' she said happily. '*That's* why I dragged you out here. It's only on nights like this that you can see it. There's too much light pollution for me to see it in England, but here...' She sighed.

'You will miss it?' Tomorrow they would fly to England. He'd further delayed his trip to Australia to help her settle into his London penthouse. The purchase of the house he was buying for her was set to be completed by the New Year.

'Very much. But I'll come back one day. When our baby's old enough… Look…' She pointed to their right, away from the Milky Way, to a cluster of stars shaped something like an hourglass. 'That's Orion.'

'How do you know so much about all this?' he marvelled.

'I have a phone app that tells me where all the stars and planets and constellations are. I've gotten to know the sky so well I rarely need to use it anymore.'

'What's the fascination?'

She pondered this before answering. 'Many things. Knowing I'm looking at the same stars humans have been looking at for millennia, wondering which stars still even exist, wondering where in the billions of stars in the Milky Way life exists…' She looked at him and smiled. 'For me, it's endlessly fascinating. I've often said that if I make it to eighty, I want to be sent off in a spaceship and travel the universe.'

'There are already trips into space. You could do one of them.'

'You have to be a gazillionaire to afford that.'

'Lena, I *am* a gazillionaire.'

She sniggered and looked back up at the sky. 'If we're still together when I'm eighty, you can buy me a rocket that will take me farther than the stratosphere.' She pointed again at the Milky Way. 'I want to go there.'

He was glad she wasn't looking at him and so didn't see the shock on his face at her, *If we're still together when I'm eighty*.

Lena thought they were in a relationship?

A burn set off in his head as he racked his brain to think why she would think this. Had *he* led her to believe this?

Konstantinos tried to think calmly. They'd become lovers four nights ago. They'd spent every waking hour together since, working on the transition from Lena's management to Sven's by day, their evenings spent dining out in the complex's restaurants and making love, and making love some more. The passion and lust between them was strong, he did not deny that—he wouldn't want to deny that; he was having the most fantastic, hedonistic, fulfilling sex of his life; he simply could not get enough of her— but at no point in any of their myriad conversations had he even intimated that they were now in a relationship. He'd made it very clear that he did not do relationships, and he knew she understood this.

And then he remembered the *if* she'd preceded her words with. *If* we're still together when I'm eighty. *If.* That implied she understood what they were currently sharing had a natural end date. It had been a flippant comment. He was reading far too much into what had been a joke.

He didn't want to put an end date on what they currently had, was prepared to enjoy the ride for as long as it lasted, but one day it would end. He knew it. Lena knew it. And when it ended, they would raise their child with the utmost respect for each other and, who knew? Maybe when she reached eighty, he would buy her that spaceship as one good friend to the other.

Feeling more settled, he pulled her closer to him at the same moment she squealed and pointed with even more vigour at the sky. *'Look!'*

Konstantinos looked. Blinked to clear his gaze. Blinked again, and then realised there was nothing wrong with his vision. The spectacle unfolding before him was no illusion.

Before his eyes the sky lit up, an arc rising of the brightest green he'd ever seen. As it rose higher and higher, more colours emerged, purples, blues, pinks, reds, undulating and streaming, the colours billowing and shifting, circling them, flashing and swaying, the entire night sky ablaze in an ethereal magic that took his breath away.

He looked at Lena. The enchantment on her face, illuminated by the dazzling light show, was a wonder in itself. And then she turned her face to his, lips pulled into the widest smile, eyes filled with joy, and the clench of his heart told him the magic she contained was more dazzling than anything nature could throw at them.

# CHAPTER TWELVE

KONSTANTINOS'S TWO-STOREY LONDON penthouse blew Lena away. Never minding the panoramic skyline view, the tall sash windows, the thick carpets her toes sank into, and tasteful modern artwork throughout the three sprawling reception rooms and five humungous bedrooms; the furnishings and adornments were exactly what she would have chosen if money was no object.

Three days they'd been holed up in this penthouse. She refused to be sad that tomorrow he would finally fly off for his much-delayed trip to Australia, not when he'd put himself under three days of sufferance from a cold and stormy English winter. Not that they'd exposed themselves to the weather. They'd been far too busy christening all the rooms of the penthouse to bother with the outside world. Oh, it made her knees weak and her pelvis burn to remember the passion with which he always made love to her. And it wasn't as if they'd be parted for long. In ten days it would be Christmas. He would fly back for her and together they would fly to Kos to spend a few days with his parents. She didn't know what came after that for them and right then, she didn't want to think about it and spoil the happiness alive in her heart.

Tonight they were going out for dinner in an underground cavern she remembered reading about when it opened but which she'd had no idea was actually owned by Konstantinos. She'd known his empire was big, but not until they'd been idly talking about it while sharing a bath had she realised the extent of it. Many of the most famous restaurants around the world had Konstantinos Siopis as the silent owner. No wonder he hated ready meals so much! She wondered how many of them she'd get to visit with him. This meal was part night out and part unofficial appraisal, which was fine by her. His empire wouldn't run itself.

With the help of a personal dresser, who'd arrived at the penthouse with five assistants armed with enough designer clothing to satisfy an army of actresses at a showbiz award, Lena was dressed in the most exquisite long-sleeved deep green satin dress that flared gently at her waist and fell to mid-calf. Beneath it, she wore black lace underwear and, for the first time in her life, sheer black thigh-high stockings. Lena was also the new proud possessor of a brand-new wardrobe of clothes, half of which were designed to accommodate her growing belly. She didn't dare think how much it had cost Konstantinos, nor how much it had cost him to chauffeur the UK's top stylist over as a surprise so she could have her hair professionally blow-dried. Since they'd become lovers, Konstantinos had treated her like a princess, and while it thrilled her to be spoilt, she couldn't shake from her mind that he'd treated Cassia like a princess, too. *In my eyes, Cassia was a princess and princesses deserved the best of everything...*

Lena was acutely aware that when Konstantinos spoke about the present, it was 'we,' and when he spoke about the future it was 'I,' and always in the abstract. With Cassia, he'd planned an entire future. With Lena, he'd mentioned nothing beyond Christmas.

She chided herself for thinking about what came next again when she'd already determined not to. The future would reveal itself in its own sweet time.

Sliding her feet into a pair of black heels she suspected she wouldn't feel safe wearing for much longer—her bump was still small but it wouldn't be for long—she reminded herself that she was having Konstantinos's child. He clearly had deep feelings for her. He clearly fancied the knickers off her. She had to remember he'd been single for over a decade for a reason and shake off the dread that rolled in her stomach whenever she thought about the woman who'd betrayed him with his own brother and broken his heart.

Konstantinos's restaurant in a quaint London suburb was nothing but an old stone barn on the outside. Appearances, as he knew very well, could be deceptive. Entering through a large oak door, to the left of the flagstone-floored hallway was a wide spiral staircase that led down to the cavern itself, a vast, dark room with discreet gold uplighting designed by his clever interior design team to give a 1930s Prohibition glamour vibe. Even the Christmas tree and sophisticated decorations matched the vibe.

They were shown to their table by the newly appointed maître d'. Not only did he trip over his own feet, he then pulled Lena's chair back with such force the leg hit the table and made the wineglasses wobble.

Konstantinos grimaced at the overly-fawning apology that followed. A maître d' was supposed be unflappable. The general manager of the restaurant had poached him from a restaurant in Mayfair. He had to wonder if the owner of that hotel had put up any kind of fight to keep him. On this performance, he'd have been glad to be rid of him.

He noticed Lena give the blundering idiot a reassuring wink as she took her seat.

'What did you do that for?' he asked as soon as they were alone.

She pulled an innocent face.

'Don't look at me like that. I saw you wink at him.'

'And?'

'Why would you reassure an idiot?'

'He's only acting like an idiot because you're here,' she replied sweetly.

'This restaurant is a favourite of celebrities and royalty,' he said, indicating the A-List Hollywood couple deep in conversation at the table closest to them. 'He should have control of himself at all times.'

She shrugged. 'Celebrities and royalty aren't his boss. You are. And you, Konstantinos Siopis, are terrifying.'

'You're exaggerating.'

'Am I…? Hmmm…?' Her generous mouth wiggled as she pretended to think before she gave another shrug. 'Nope. Not exaggerating. You're terrifying. When you interviewed me for Thom's job, I was so frightened I nearly put an adult nappy on, just in case.'

He laughed. 'You hid your fear well.'

Her eyes danced with amusement. 'Want to know how I did it?'

'Tell me.'

She leaned closer and dropped her voice. 'By imagining you naked.'

'You didn't?'

Her eyes gleamed. 'I totally did. And let me tell you, my imagination had *nothing* on reality.'

'What did your imagination get wrong?'

'I underestimated the muscularity and hairiness of your chest for a start.'

'And?' he prompted.

Her ankle rubbed against his calf and the gleam in her eyes deepened. 'I *totally* underestimated the size of your—'

'Are we ready to order?' A young waiter apparated at their side. Or seemed to apparate. Konstantinos was very tempted to tell him to apparate off.

Gritting his teeth to fight the arousal the beautiful woman now sitting with serene innocence opposite him had deliberately induced, he attempted a smile to prove he was not a terrifying ogre who reduced his staff to blundering messes.

From the widening of the waiter's eyes, his attempt was futile. Full credit to him, though; he laid their drinks down and took their order with the polite professionalism Konstantinos demanded of all his staff.

Alone again, Lena raised her glass of alcohol-free wine and gave a wide smile. 'Now, isn't this fun?'

His blood thick with desire, he soaked in the beauty no army of professionals could improve on. Even now, dressed to the nines and as ravishing as he'd ever seen her, he could only think that Lena looked her best wearing nothing at all.

By the time they made it back to the penthouse, Konstantinos was just about ready to explode. Lena had spent the entire evening torturing him. His idea of making the visit an unofficial appraisal of the restaurant had been forgotten the moment she rubbed her ankle against him. Her torture had been subtle. Anyone watching would have seen nothing but a beautiful woman gazing adoringly into her lover's eyes. What they wouldn't have seen was the way her arms pressed suggestively against her breasts, the way her gaze often drifted slowly up and down his chest as if she were mentally undressing him, how she licked her lips suggestively... They definitely wouldn't have seen the lascivious knowing in her eyes at the effects of her silent seduction. She'd known damned well what she was doing, and when they'd gotten back in his car and he'd pulled her to him, she'd calmly crossed her legs, held his hand firmly on her lap and refused to let it wander any farther.

'You're driving me crazy,' he'd muttered, to which she'd given that serene, innocent smile and said, 'Am I?'

He'd growled, envisaging the moment the door of his penthouse closed. And now that moment had arrived, but as soon as he tried to pull her into his arms, she skipped out of his reach with a throaty laugh and headed up the stairs.

Shrugging his suit jacket off and dropping it on the stairs, he reached the bedroom ripping his tie off… Only to find the room empty and the bathroom door closed.

Breathing deeply, he closed his eyes and tried to get a handle on the desire zinging so deeply in his veins.

Another deep breath and he undid the top three buttons of his shirt and pulled it over his head. He was just stepping out of his trousers, butt naked, when the bathroom door opened.

Mouth running dry, he straightened. His erection sprang back into a totem pole.

Her dress had been removed. But only her dress.

In a cloud of delicious, seductive perfume, breasts bouncing gently beneath the confines of the sheer black lace bra, hips swaying, she stalked towards him.

The extra inches of height her heels gave her meant when she stood before him, she almost reached his chin. Tilting her face up, she smiled. And then she pushed him onto the bed.

Lena had no idea what had gotten into her. She'd never set out to drive Konstantinos out of his mind. It had been seeing the darkening of his eyes when she'd teased him about how she'd imagined him naked that had started it; knowing that beneath the dapper dark suit arousal had pooled, and that she had caused it. It had been thrilling. Exciting. And it had turned her on as much as him.

Staring at him now, at the beautiful vampiric face contorted with his desire for her, her heart a pulsing ragged mess, her insides molten, she realised she loved him. That that was what this seduction was all about. She loved Konstantinos. Madly. Passionately. She wanted him. Madly. Passionately. She wanted to give him the same pleasure he took such pleasure in giving her. Worship him. Devour him. Make him hers forever...

She pounced.

Straddling his abdomen, she kissed him deeply, savagely, unleashing the last of the emotions she hadn't even realised she'd been hiding from them both. It was too late for self-preservation. Her heart belonged to him now.

Wrenching her mouth from his, Lena gazed into his hooded eyes, feeding on the hunger she found in them.

A noise like a groan came from his throat.

She kissed him again, harder. He returned it with equal ferocity. And then she wrenched her mouth away again and rubbed her cheek against the stubbled jaw before grazing her lips, tongue and teeth down his neck. There was not a single bit of Konstantinos she didn't love, she thought dreamily as she licked a brown nipple and felt him shudder. Her nails dragged through the thick hair on his chest and abdomen, the soft black hair the only part of him that was soft. Everything else was hard and yet so incredibly smooth, and she loved every part of it. Loved him, this complicated, sexy man with the beautiful green eyes and crooked smile and generous heart that had been encased in ice for far too long. Loved, loved, loved him. Loved eliciting one of his rare smiles. Loved eliciting one of his even rarer laughs. Loved the groans of pleasure coming from his mouth as she licked the velvet head of his erection and then ran her tongue down the long, thick length.

Lena had never been shy about showing her desire for him before, but this was a whole new level, Konstantinos thought hazily, his eyes flickering shut as she gripped the base and covered him with the whole of her mouth. This was nothing she hadn't done to him before, but…this was something else.

He moaned her name. *Theos*, this must be heaven.

The pace of her movements was strengthening. The rush of pleasure was intensifying. He was so close…

Too close. He wanted to touch her. Taste her… *Theos*, he could not get enough of her taste. Of her.

Lifting his head, he threaded his fingers through her silky hair and gently pulled her head back.

She looked at him with confused eyes drugged with desire. Her lips were shiny with the moisture her mouth had created. 'What's wrong?'

'Come here,' he said thickly. 'I need to kiss you.'

She crawled up his chest. As soon as their lips fused together, he rolled her onto her back, then pinned her flat so he could get his fill of her, not just her scent and taste but the heat she exuded, the throaty moans that turned into gasps when he removed her bra and cupped her breasts, the cries of pleasure when he flicked his tongue over the cherry peaks. Her sensitivity to his touch never failed to thrill him, feed him. He wanted more. He wanted *everything*.

Lena had become a mass of nerve endings. Every part of her was on fire, Konstantinos's hands trailing scorch marks as he peeled her knickers off, the flames burning brighter when he flickered his tongue up to the delicate folds between her thighs and then teased it over the nub of her pleasure. And then he stopped teasing.

The molten heat inside her began to bubble at the pure pleasure he was endowing her with, each lap of his tongue driving her closer and closer to the release she craved, and all she could do was grip the nearest pillow tightly. 'God, yes,' she moaned, thrashing her head and arching her pelvis in fervent encouragement. 'Yes, Tinos, yes. Oh, yes.'

The heat was rising, her climax building, but just

as she got the first sense of the telltale quickening, he cruelly moved his mouth away from where she so desperately wanted it to stay. Before she could protest, he was sliding over her and then he was sliding inside her, and her protest died into nothing as he filled her completely in one hard thrust.

There was no savouring. No slow, sensual buildup. Not tonight.

Lust-filled eyes fixed on hers, Konstantinos pushed her knees back and, his chest brushing against the tips of her breasts, pounded into her with a passionate savagery that fired her carnal responses as much as the ferocious concentration on his face. Her nerve endings caught fire and then she was crying out his name, begging him for more, more, more as the molten reached the brim, blood rushed in her veins, and suddenly she was drowning in wave upon wave upon wave of unadulterated bliss carried along by the roar of Konstantinos's own climax.

Lena had lain spooned in Konstantinos's arms for what felt like hours, unable to sleep, when their baby woke up and decided to have a party in her belly. Konstantinos must have felt it beneath the hand splayed on her stomach for he stroked it gently. She'd thought he was asleep.

She couldn't hide from her own thoughts anymore. The secret fears she'd tried so hard to keep locked away were flooding her, and now the greatest fear spilled out in a whispered, 'What happens between us after Christmas?'

She knew she wasn't imagining the tension that tautened his body.

Her words hung in the air for an impossible length of time, until his body relaxed and he rubbed his cheek affectionately into her hair. 'We will work something out.'

She kissed his arm and slowly breathed out her relief.

The wound from his brother and fiancée's betrayal cut so deep that she didn't know if Konstantinos would ever allow himself to love her, but she knew he had feelings for her that went beyond amazing sex. He showed it in so many ways, and, though she feared she was being foolish, she couldn't stop her heart expanding with hope that one day...

The swimming in Konstantinos's head alternated hot and cold, a mixture of strengthening emotions coursing through him. Slowly, much slower than it usually took, her breaths evened out. The hand holding his went limp. Finally, Konstantinos felt able to move his head back and expel the longest breath of his life. Anger filled his next inhale, although whether it was directed at Lena or himself he couldn't determine.

He knew what her question meant.

He knew, too, what had felt so different about their lovemaking that night. It was what he'd felt from Lena that had been different. Raw emotion. She'd given the entirety of herself to him.

And now she wanted to know what came next for them.

There was no *them*. Not in the way she wanted. She should know that. She *did* know that.

He had told Lena, explicitly, that he did not do relationships. While he conceded that what they currently shared could be construed as a form of relationship, the fact remained that if not for their baby, neither of them would be in this bed. He was not prepared to commit himself to anyone and she knew it; the most he was prepared to do, and only because of the baby, was take things one day at a time, which was a hell of a lot more than he'd been prepared to do before. He didn't know how long that one day at a time would last. He didn't want to know.

He strongly suspected Lena wanted to know. She wanted to plan a future with him. He could feel it in his bones.

Future. A word that filled him with sulphur.

He'd done that whole future thing before and look how that had turned out. Betrayed. His trust destroyed. He would never put himself in that position again.

# CHAPTER THIRTEEN

THERE WAS A heaviness in Lena's stomach from the moment she woke, a sick sense of dread. Konstantinos was leaving soon for Australia.

Clambering out of the empty bed, she pulled her kimono-style silk dressing gown on and went off in search of him.

She found him in the dining room, a variety of breakfast foods around him, reading something on his phone. He looked up as she entered and smiled.

'You should have woken me,' she accused, trying not to sound tearful.

'I didn't have the heart.' He shifted his chair back so she could sit on his lap. 'You were fast asleep. I was about to come and wake you.'

She sank onto his muscular thighs and kissed him. 'When do you need to leave?'

'In thirty minutes.'

She sighed and leaned her head back so their cheeks could press together. He was so freshly shaven that not even the slightest stubble grazed her skin.

He'd be back in a week, she reminded herself. That wasn't so long. It hadn't sounded long before. It had sounded short. Now her chest felt as if it had been injected with ice; Konstantinos flying to the other side of the world a stark reality.

She tried hard to hide her dejection. She didn't want his last memory to be of her mopey. 'All packed?'

'Yes. My cases have already been taken to the car. Are you still planning to visit your family later?'

She nodded. 'I'll wait until you've left and then get myself sorted.' They'd exchanged the same frequency of video calls and messaging, but her family was unaware she was already in England. She would tell them everything today.

'Call the concierge when you're ready. They will provide a car for you… You are sure you're familiar with how to use the concierge service?'

'Yep. Dial nine.'

He kissed her temple and tapped her thigh as a signal for her to get off his lap.

Sighing again, Lena slid into the chair beside his and surveyed the array of food spread out on the table. She had no appetite. While Konstantinos poured himself another of the strong Greek coffees he virtually overdosed on each morning, her tongue burned with the unspoken plea for him not to go.

'I have given some thought to what you asked me last night,' he said conversationally.

Her heart jolted.

Konstantinos had spent the morning drafting a

speech in his head. He'd woken so early the sun—
and that there actually was any sun was the only
good thing about being in England in December—
hadn't even attempted to rise. Leaving Lena sleeping, he'd worked out in his gym for an hour. By the
time he'd finished, sweat had poured off him and
the anger that had gripped him in the wake of her
unwanted question and the implications he'd sensed
underlying it had diminished enough for him to think
rationally.

He didn't want to lose what they had. The sex was
just too good to willingly give that up. He needed to
strike a balance between making his feelings clear
and not hurting her. Hurting her was the last thing
he wanted to do. His prepared speech would do the
trick, and allow him to fly to Australia without anything hanging over them.

'I should tell you now my post-Christmas schedule is incredibly busy and will be so until a few
weeks before your due date. Once the baby is born
then, naturally, things will change and I will work
my schedule so that I'm away on business for shorter
periods. This will leave me with more free time to
be a father and give you the support you need.' This
was something they had already discussed but he
thought it worth reiterating.

'As you know, I am not a man prepared to commit
to a relationship.' He stared at her intently, willing
her to absorb what he was saying and not just hear
it. 'But I am prepared to make a form of commitment to you. I appreciate that it isn't the full commit-

ment I suspect you are hoping for, but it is a solution I think will suit us both very well without putting unnecessary obligations on each other, other than in respects to our child.'

Something flashed in her eyes but she didn't attempt to speak.

'I propose making you my official plus-one. When I attend functions that require a partner, I will fly you out to me. Obviously, this will have to be paused when the doctors deem you no longer safe to fly and until you are fully recovered from the birth. Once you are recovered, I will hire a nanny to travel with you. Also, I will provide you with a personal allowance, much more than the maintenance we've already spoken of.'

She merely raised an eyebrow and gave a sharp nod, silently encouraging him to continue.

Aware his time was limited, Konstantinos hit his stride. 'Being the mother of my child automatically makes you important to me.' This was something he needed to make clear. Lena was important to him and he wanted her to know it. 'We will be co-parents who share a bed for as long as the desire between us lasts. Once it comes to its natural end, we will simply be co-parents and, I am sure, great friends. We can decide then whether you will continue acting as my plus-one.'

Looking at him with thoughtful eyes, Lena poured herself a glass of orange juice and sipped from it before cradling it in her hands. 'Okay, let me make sure I'm clear on this.'

He looked at his watch. Fifteen minutes until he had to leave. 'Sure.'

'You will make pockets of time in your busy schedule to spend in the UK with me and the baby.'

'I would also like some of those pockets of time to be spent in Kos. It is my home. I want our child to know my parents and my heritage.'

'That's reasonable.'

Konstantinos relaxed.

'While you and I are lovers,' she continued summarising, 'those pockets of time will be spent together under the same roof, and when it comes to its natural end, you will collect our child and spend that quality time alone, possibly with me joining you for the odd day out or meal so our child can see his or her parents getting on fabulously well?'

He inclined his head.

'Have you thought about buying me a home in Kos? It might make things easier if we decide to part company as lovers while we're spending quality time there.'

Hadn't he known from the beginning how smart this woman was? 'That does make sense.'

'Doesn't it?' she agreed brightly. 'And, to clarify, while we are lovers, you will fly me out to wherever you are in the world when you need a plus-one, like a quasi-official escort, *and* give me an allowance as payment?'

About to agree that she'd described it all perfectly, her final two words took a moment to penetrate. 'I did not call it payment.'

'No.' She shook her head and gave him a look of such sweetness that a pulse began to throb in his head, a warning that something was off. 'My mistake. You're right. You didn't call it that.'

She had another sip of her juice, her velvet brown eyes continuing to appraise him thoughtfully.

Her silence unnerved him. Her whole demeanour did. The pulse in his head throbbed even harder. 'Your thoughts on my proposal?'

'Oh, it makes perfect sense,' she said musingly. 'If you're a complete psychopath.'

It was witnessing Konstantinos's jaw drop that tipped Lena over the edge.

She'd listened to him deliver what was clearly a prepared speech with something close to disbelief. She'd never expected a marriage proposal or anything even close to one, but this was something else. This was cold. Clinical. And deliberately so. If she wasn't carrying his child, he would be ending it right now, would already have ordered her bags be packed. And why? Because she'd asked for the impossible. For him to think beyond tomorrow. To think of *her* beyond tomorrow.

Throughout, her pride had whispered to her, telling her not to react, to keep calm, to thank him for his reasoned thoughts and then politely tell him that this wasn't something she could agree to, and end it herself.

Her pride could go to hell. And so could Konstantinos.

The hand she'd clenched so tightly around the

glass, the hand she'd fought so hard to stop betraying her inner turmoil by trembling, took control of her and flung the remaining juice at him.

In a flash, he'd shoved his chair back and shot to his feet. 'What the hell, Lena?' he snarled. The juice had landed on his chest, soaked into his white shirt, splatters of it dripping off his neck and chin.

'What the hell, *Lena*?' she mimicked with a cry, slamming the glass on the table and giving it a good shove before shooting to her own feet. 'What do you think I am? Some kind of escort that you can fly out to you at your convenience?'

Swearing loudly, he swiped his chin with the back of his hand. 'Do not twist what I said. If my proposal is not to your liking, you only have to say no.'

She nearly snatched the glass back so she could throw it at him. 'No! I say no. Never. I will not prostitute myself for you.'

His furious face contorted. 'Prostitute yourself? How on earth did you come up with that?'

'Did you not hear yourself? You would have agreed to buy me anything I asked for, wouldn't you? And all in exchange for me keeping your bed warm as and when *you* decide, and with absolutely everything on your terms. Well, forget it. I won't do it. If you can't respect me then you certainly don't get to sleep with me.'

'Of course I respect you! I offered you more than I have offered anyone!'

'Oh, forgotten about Cassia, have you? Forgotten all the plans you made with her?'

'That was different.'

'How?'

'You know how, but in any case, this has nothing to do with her.'

'It has everything to do with her and you know it. I am not Cassia, and I am insulted you think I'm anything like her.'

Outrage further darkened the features now leaning into her. 'I have *never* compared you to her.'

'You've compared every woman you've ever met with her!' she shouted back, stretching her neck so she could get into his face as much as he was getting into hers, close enough that every angry exhale he made landed on her skin like a blow. 'It's always in the back of your mind, isn't it? That we're only out for what we can get from you? The only thing I ever wanted from you, Tinos, was *you*.'

'I told you from the start that I don't do relationships.'

'We're having a baby!' she screamed, now completely divorced from the composure her pride had tried so hard to force on her.

'Yes, and that's the only reason we're even having this discussion.'

'Have you not considered for the slightest moment that it's the same for me? That you're not the only one who's backed away from relationships? You know I've been celibate for *years* but having our baby and being with you has forced me to look at why that was because I damned well didn't stay single consciously.'

The pulse on his jaw throbbed, a sign it sliced her heart to recognise. 'The guilt you still carry because you walked away without a physical scratch,' he said tightly. 'A family is the thing your sister most wanted.'

She laughed manically. 'See? You already knew the answer. In some ways, you already know me better than I know myself. I bet that terrifies you, doesn't it, that you've gotten close enough to understand me?'

She laughed again at the clenching of his pulsing jaw. He knew her but she knew him equally well, and it was that knowing that destroyed her. 'But yes, you're right, and I'm pretty sure the fact you were my boss and a heavily committed bachelor played some small part in my letting myself go with you because those things made you unobtainable. And if it wasn't for our baby there is no way I would have slept with you again no matter how badly I wanted to. God, Tinos, you would not believe how my heart would practically explode when a message from you pinged in my inbox, and then when I found I was pregnant with your child...'

It struck her then, the hopelessness of it all.

The anger draining from her, Lena cradled her belly and took a step back, her first step away from him.

'It changed everything for me,' she said simply. 'I was terrified of your reaction. You know that. But always there was this small part of me that dared to hope that once our baby was born and you were satisfied he or she was yours, that you and I could at least try, for the baby's sake. I knew it was a pipe dream but it was still there, but I know now that it is never going to happen. You won't let it happen. Your offer…' She shook her head and willed the tears she could feel burning the backs of her eyes to stay put just that bit longer. 'It isn't just a disrespectful insult to me but a disrespectful insult to *us* and everything we've found together. Our baby might have forced us together but what we've shared is all us, Tinos. You and me. You've made me the happiest I've ever been in my life and I know I've made you happy, too, and you're throwing us away. You gutless *coward*.'

Her *coward* was whispered but Konstantinos felt the impact of it as hard as if she'd shouted it laced with barbed wire. It only fired the fury that had run amok in his veins since she'd hurled the contents of her glass at him and thrown his offer in his face.

With slow deliberation, he looked at his watch and then looked back at her ashen face. 'It is time for me to leave,' he said with equally slow deliberation that contained all the bite of his anger. He did not think he had ever felt such loathing for another human being. That Lena, of all people, should twist his own words and actions and accuse him of disrespect when he had given her more damned respect than he'd ever given anyone, enraged him, and that she was now standing there with the air of a martyr only added fuel to this.

Her face pinched on itself but she raised her chin. 'Good.'

'I think it best my solicitor deal with you with regards to the house purchase.'

Contempt flashed in her eyes. 'I just bet you do.'

He glared at her with equal contempt.

Her chin remained risen. 'Have you an intermediary in mind for me to keep you informed about anything baby related?'

'Considering you never had any intention of me knowing about the baby until it was born, I am astounded you would think to ask.' Placing his phone in his pocket, he patted it. 'Message me. But only about the baby. I have no interest in anything else.'

Konstantinos left the penthouse with the burn of Lena's disdain still scorching his skin.

Lena gazed out her parents' kitchen window at the birds making themselves at home on the bird table her mum had made when Lena was still at school. She'd always loved their garden. Such happy memories. If she concentrated hard enough, she could see herself and Heidi practising their handstands and cartwheels, each determined to best the other. She supposed they'd had their own form of sibling rivalry after all.

Footsteps sounded behind her. A hand touched her shoulder; a kiss dropped into her hair. 'Are you okay, *älskling*?'

She pressed her head against her mum's. 'I will be.'

She had to be okay. For her baby's sake. It was for her baby's sake that she had forced herself to eat these past five days. It was for her baby's sake that she'd moved out of Konstantinos's penthouse and taken up her parents' and sister's heartfelt insistence that she stay with them. She hadn't had much choice when her dad returned from a mystery trip with a fold-up bed that must have cost more than a decent permanent bed, and rearranged the living room furniture to fit it in.

They knew everything. Once Konstantinos had gone, she'd dragged herself to the bedroom, pulled some clothes on, and got the concierge to arrange a driver to take her to her family. Her intention to only tell them about the baby without giving any details had been as good as her intention of never falling in love with Konstantinos. It had all spilled out. The only details she'd spared them had been of the actual conception itself. In many ways, it had been cathartic. In many others, reliving it all only made her despair grow. She'd handed her heart to a man who didn't want it.

Her family had been brilliant. She'd known all along that they would support her but what she hadn't comprehended was how much she *needed* their support. Their love. As for Heidi… The joy that had sparkled in her eyes when Lena had lifted her top for her to see the bump had put to rest her fears that this would be another kick in the teeth to a woman who had already lost so much.

She wished she had her sister's strength. She'd tried. Tried her hardest to save her tears until night came and the house fell silent with sleep. She was trying now, as she watched the birds feeding and the images of the two young girls practising their gymnastics continued to flicker before her filling eyes.

So much loss. So much pain.

'Mum?' she whispered.

'Yes, *älskling*?'

'I miss him.'

When the tears spilled out, she couldn't fight them, could only cling tightly to her mum and soak her jumper with her tears, praying her mum spoke the truth when she softly said time always healed.

Lena feared her heart had shattered into too many pieces to ever heal.


Konstantinos finished his Scotch. The temptation to pour himself another was strong but he resisted. He'd drunk more than he would usually consume in recent days. But not wine. For some reason the smell of wine currently turned his stomach. He'd put his hand over his glass to stop the waiter from pouring it during a meal with his senior Australian management team earlier that evening.

He'd only drunk more Scotch than usual because his chest felt so damn cold and hollow. He couldn't think what was wrong with him. Here he was, in the midst of a roasting Australian summer and he felt none of the usual benefits.

His phone buzzed. His heart thumped as it had done with every buzz since he'd landed here. He had no idea why that was, either.

He reached to his hotel suite's bedside table for it. A message from his mother. This time his heart clenched. She wanted to know what she should buy Lena for Christmas. Like most of their compatriots, the Siopis family exchanged gifts on New Year's Day but his mother had been researching how the Brits did it and learned they exchanged theirs, like a growing number of Greeks, on Christmas Day itself. His kind-hearted mother wanted Lena to enjoy some of her own traditions.

He sighed heavily and reached for the Scotch after all, took a drink and then relayed the message he should have told his parents days ago: that Lena wouldn't be joining them.

Why had he put it off?

*Gutless coward.*

He poured himself another drink, this time to drown the sound of Lena's contempt from his mind.

# CHAPTER FOURTEEN

AFTER MIDNIGHT MASS with his parents, Konstantinos sat at the front terrace of the family restaurant that had been a part of his whole life and gazed up at the stars. How had he never seen them before? His formative years spent living in Kos's mountains, at a location where tourists flocked to watch the sunset, and not once had he lifted his eyes upward and seen what was above him. The night sky had simply been there.

He wondered if Lena was outside looking up, too.

He couldn't stop thinking about her. The harder he tried, the worse it got. A Lena-sized infection of the mind. And now it was officially Christmas Day and she was thousands of miles away, her silence as deep a chasm as the distance between them.

'What are you doing out here?' His father pulled up a chair beside him.

'Looking at the stars.'

They sat in comfortable silence for a long while. That was something Konstantinos had always appreciated about his father. He never felt the need to fill silences.

'Is something on your mind, son?'

He'd thought too soon.

He tried to smile. 'Nothing important.'

There was more silence, then, 'Is it that Lena?'

There was nothing malicious about his father's question but still he found himself bristling at her being referred to as *that* Lena.

Instead of answering, he asked a question of his own. 'Why did you and Mama take Theo's side?'

His father sighed. 'Tinos... We didn't take sides. We couldn't. You are both our sons.'

It was nothing he didn't already know. Nothing that, in truth, needed explaining. But it had only been since hearing Lena so vehemently take his part that he'd realised how deeply his parents' neutrality had affected him, that it bit to alternate Christmases and other significant events. That Theo and Cassia still enjoyed a close relationship with them.

His father gave another heavy sigh and reached for his hand to squeeze it. 'Theodoros behaved terribly to you. I have never condoned it. If you had asked me to choose between the two of you, I would have been duty bound to choose you, and I thank you for not forcing that choice on us. I know it has been hard for you, but Tinos, it is time to let it go.'

'Yes,' he agreed, surprising them both. 'It is.'

His father squeezed his hand again. 'Cassia was never right for you. She would have made you unhappy.'

'I know.'

That startled him. 'You do?'

'Yes. She is inherently selfish.' Lena had shown him that simply by being Lena. Lena didn't have a selfish bone in her body.

'She is,' his father agreed. 'That is why she is better for your brother. They cancel each other's selfishness out.'

A burst of unexpected laughter flew from Konstantinos's mouth but it died quickly in his throat, caught by a burst of something else, something that swelled in a wave and ripped through him before he could find the presence to clamp it down and smother it.

There was nothing he could do to stop the great sobs from racking him but cover his face in a futile attempt to stem the tears and admit the truth to himself.

The coldness in his chest the Australian heat had failed to cure was caused by him severing himself from the only pure sunshine of his life. Lena. She was *his* sun. His life had revolved around her since she'd walked into the meeting room for the interview and the sun's rays had beamed through the window and cast her in gold.

He'd been too blind to recognise it.

He loved her. God help him, he'd fallen in love with her, and he'd driven her away and hurt her and turned the love she had for him into contempt.

A meaty arm slipped around his back and pulled him into an embrace that only made his sobs louder.

'Whatever you have done to drive this Lena away,

you can fix it,' his father said quietly once the sobs had quietened. 'I know you can.'

His father's steadfast faith in him brought no consolation. His father didn't know the depth of the pain he'd caused her.

He'd lost her. Lost his sun.

And it was all his own fault.

Lena was about to leave the hotel room when her phone rang.

'Did you forget one?' she asked, laughing. She'd not long finished a marathon early-morning video call with her family where they'd all opened their Christmas presents together, although this year she'd gotten them to open her presents for her. It was a tradition they'd formed when she'd first started working at the Ice Hotel. Her family had been disappointed when she'd told them they'd have to do the same this year—they'd thought that seeing as she was no longer working there, she'd be free to spend the day with them—but had understood the commitment she'd already made and wasn't willing to rescind, no matter the personal cost.

But there was no answer.

'Mum?'

Then she heard it. The sound of crying.

'Mum?' she repeated, alarmed. 'What's wrong? Is it Heidi?'

Her dad took the phone. 'Sorry, love, your mum's in shock. We all are.'

'What's happened?'

'Your mum checked her banking app—you know what she's like.' Lena did know. Her mum checked their bank account each morning like most people checked their social media feeds. It didn't surprise her in the least that she would do it on Christmas Day, too. 'Well…' Her dad cleared his throat. 'At some point since she checked it yesterday morning, we've had a million pounds deposited into it.'

'I'm sorry, what?'

'A million pounds.' He cleared his throat again. 'The crediting account was K Siopis. The reference was Merry Christmas.'

Lena walked from her hotel at the top of the winding, sweeping road that cut through the town until she found the name of the restaurant she was looking for. Having arrived late in the evening, the town had been alive with Christmas lights and thrumming with people and groups of children singing Christmas carols. Now the town, as pretty by day as by night, lay silent.

She remembered Konstantinos telling her that you could open a door in the restaurant's kitchen and be in the family home, which his parents adamantly refused to move from. Now all she had to do was find the other entrance to it.

The main restaurant door was locked so she climbed the steps to its L-shaped terrace and stopped for a moment to admire the view. It truly was spectacular. No wonder the place was a Mecca for sunset worshippers. Laid out before her, as far as the eye could see, the Aegean Sea, gleaming under the brightening skies, as picture perfect as anything a landscape artist could compose, the few boats sailing on it mere daubs of white paint.

A peal of female laughter made her close her eyes to the vista. In truth, it hadn't been the view she'd paused for but a moment to gather herself before she saw him. So much hurt unbearably, but Konstantinos's leaving her to make her own arrangements to get here hurt the most. She had no way of knowing if she was too early or too late.

She followed the laughter around the terrace corner.

Two glamorous women, maybe a decade older than her mum, were standing by a huge plant pot, deep in expressive conversation, smoking. The shorter one spotted Lena first and immediately elbowed the other, who frowned and yelled out something to her she didn't understand.

Hesitantly, she inched farther forward. 'Excuse me,' she called, wishing she'd done a crash course in Greek. 'Speak English?'

The taller one's frown deepened. Her eyes dropped to Lena's belly and then her eyebrows rose. With the same hesitation that Lena had spoken, she said, 'Lena?'

She nodded.

The woman's shock was so transparent that Lena instantly knew she'd made a massive mistake. She wasn't supposed to be here. But before she could apologise for intruding and go find somewhere private to lick her humiliated wounds, the woman crushed her cigarette underfoot, gabbled something urgently to the other woman then hurled herself at Lena.

In the blink of an eye, Lena found herself enveloped in a cloud of perfumed smoke, the welcome so profusive and heartfelt that tears stabbed the backs of her retinas.

'You came,' the woman finally said when she decided to let Lena breathe again. Rubbing the tops of Lena's arms, she smiled tremulously. 'You came.'

She blinked back the tears and nodded before quietly asking the woman she was certain was Konstantinos's mother, 'Am I still welcome?'

The woman's jaw dropped as if she'd been asked the most obtuse question in the world. 'Eh?' And then she gave her another powerful hug that answered more potently than mere words could that Lena was more than welcome in her home.

When she next released her, the other woman had reappeared on the terrace with two women of around Lena's age and four men. The tallest of the men stared at her as if she were a ghost.

She could have thrown up on the spot. Luckily, his mother clasped her hand tightly, and Lena clung to her for support as she was brought forward for introductions. Names were thrown at her. Arms were thrown around her...all but Konstantinos, who stood back wordlessly.

Konstantinos watched the scene unfold before him as if he was watching a movie. It didn't feel real.

Lena had appeared like a mirage. If he blinked, she was sure to vanish.

But she didn't vanish, and when his mother dragged her inside, he followed with everyone else, then watched with that same observer feeling as another chair was taken into the dining room, where the Christmas bread already had pride of place on the table, placemats and cutlery rearranged to fit another place setting, heard the loud laughter when his mother produced a surprise packet of English Christmas Crackers and placed them around the table, too. He watched his family fuss around Lena, his aunt stroke her hair, his father hand her a drink, his cousin offer her an almond biscuit, the other cousin then take her hand and drag her off to see the Christmas tree that stood proudly in the living room.

His uncle came over to speak to him once everyone else had congregated in the living room. He recalled nothing of the conversation other than the panic that grabbed his chest when he looked again to where Lena had just been sitting and found she'd disappeared. It took a long time for the beats of his heart to regain any kind of regularity after she returned, her hand held by his mother, a necklace that hadn't been there before hung around her neck. From the way Lena kept pressing her hand to it, she was obviously enamoured.

'She doesn't bite,' his father said, standing beside him.

'What?'

'Lena. She doesn't bite.'

He tried to smile but couldn't make his mouth form anything. 'She isn't here to see me.' That much was clear. Other than that first clash of eyes, she hadn't looked in his direction or gotten within three feet of him.

She was here, he knew, because she'd given her word.

He still couldn't quite believe it.

'She's been here two hours and not looked at you once that I've noticed. No one avoids looking at someone for so long if they don't feel something for them.'

'She hates me.'

'Hate is a feeling. Your mother often hates me. Talk to her.'

He took a long breath and nodded.

His opportunity came shortly after, when his mother, aunt and one of his cousins bustled off back to the terrace to get another of their nicotine fixes and his father, uncle and grandfather went into the kitchen to check on the food. Konstantinos fixed his stare on Rena, his cousin currently practising her pidgin English on Lena. She noticed, murmured something he couldn't hear, and disappeared, leaving them alone.

*Theos*, he could hardly breathe.

The beats of Lena's heart went into overdrive. She'd hoped the number of people crammed into the modest home meant she could avoid Konstantinos until it was polite for her to leave. She didn't want to make small talk with him. It was torture enough to share the same air as he did, knowing he hated her very existence.

She wished she could hate him. Wished she didn't feel so bereft without him. Wished she didn't long for him to pull her into his arms and tell her he was sorry, that he hadn't meant any of it, that he loved her.

She wished she could plug her ears from her thoughts.

He hovered before her.

Self-conscious, she crossed her legs and turned her head to the door. If she willed it hard enough, someone would come in and save her.

'You came,' he said, unwittingly using the same words his mother had. The difference was his mother had been delighted to see her.

'I made a promise,' she said shortly. 'Although it's pretty clear they weren't expecting me. Thanks for letting me know you'd cancelled for me.'

'I didn't think you would still want to come.'

'Don't you mean you hoped? Well, don't worry, I won't outstay my welcome.'

'From the way they have all taken to you, you could never do that. If I'd known, I would have arranged all your transport and everything for you.'

'Christmas dinner is not baby related and so comes under the *not interested* category,' she stated acidly.

'About that.' She heard him take a deep breath and felt her insides shrivel. God, no, don't let him find more words to hurt her with. 'Lena—'

'Before I forget,' she interrupted. 'My parents say thank you for their Christmas present.'

There was a long pause. 'Please tell them it is my pleasure.'

She raised a shoulder. It was the only movement she was now capable of making. Her entire insides hadn't just shrivelled but clenched into a tight ball. That money would make a massive difference to their lives, especially to Heidi's. They'd be able to move, buy a much more spacious house where wheel-chairs weren't prone to getting stuck.

A gong clanged out.

Konstantinos swore under his breath. It was his father's traditional Christmas method of announc-ing dinner was ready.

Lena had avoided his stare for the entire conver-sation.

Lena ate as much as she could of the roast lamb, spinach and cheese pie, and the vast array of vege-tables and salads that accompanied it. She pulled her cracker with Konstantinos's grandfather and wore the paper hat that fell out of it and which all the Siopises seemed completely bemused by but fol-lowed suit with their own cracker hats. She ate her share of the sweet treats that followed. She tried to help with the clearing up but was shooed out of the dining room and banned from the kitchen. She sat with Konstantinos's cousins and helped them with the English they were determined to improve, and then she went back into the dining room for the traditional Siopis game of cards, a game she'd never heard of and which involved much shouting and swearing and accusations of cheating. She ate more of the never-ending stream of food brought out to the table. She exchanged amused looks with Konstantinos's mother when her father-in-law's head fell back mid-card game and he started snoring. And all the while, her insides clenched ever tighter and the pain in her heart became more than she could endure.

She didn't know it, but Grandfather's snoring was her means of escape. The uncle declared it time to get his father home and Lena used the distraction of all the kisses and embraces to quietly slip away with them.

Out in the cool, fresh air, she wrapped her jacket tighter around herself and took a moment to just breathe.

That had been the hardest day of her life. Every minute had been agony.

Never again. She couldn't. Couldn't be in a room with Konstantinos and smile and laugh and pretend she was having a great time when the bleeding of her heart threatened to drown her.

She hid in the shadows until the uncle's car had passed and then set off. Ten minutes, that was all it would take to walk to the hotel. She would be safe then.

Safe from herself.

Safe from throwing herself at Konstantinos and begging him to come back to her.

\* \* \*

Konstantinos spotted Lena's absence immediately.

'Where's Lena?' he called out sharply.

Everyone looked around, as if she could be hiding under a rug or behind a door.

Even as they searched the house calling her name, he knew she'd gone. She'd slipped out with his uncle and grandfather without saying goodbye. He yanked his phone out of his back pocket and called his uncle.

Why would she do that? That wasn't Lena. She would never just disappear without saying goodbye and thanking his parents for their hospitality. She just wouldn't.

His uncle finally answered.

'Is Lena with you?'

'No. Why?'

He disconnected the call and, for the first time since he'd left her in London, dialled Lena's number. It went straight to voice mail.

His phone rang. His uncle calling him back. He thrust the phone at his mother. 'You talk to him. I'm going to find her.'

There was no sign of her on the terrace.

He hurled himself down the steps and onto the street. The Christmas lights were illuminating the town in their festive colours. Illuminating the street.

Which direction had she gone?

He tried to think calmly, no easy feat when panic had gripped him so completely.

Why the hell hadn't he forced her to talk earlier?

No, why had he admitted defeat when the dinner gong had rung? *Theos*, all he'd needed to say were three little words. *I am sorry*. More than anything, those were the words he needed to say to her. He didn't think he'd find peace or sleep again until he'd said them.

There were no hotels to the right of the restaurant so she must have turned left, he determined, his legs already setting off as the thought formed. He knew she was staying at a hotel here; he'd overheard her telling Rena.

Upping his pace to a run, he flew up the winding road, rounding yet another bend until he spotted the figure in the distance, close to the town's giant Christmas tree.

'Lena!' he shouted. Tried to shout. It came out as a croak. Still running, closing in on her with every stride, he shouted her name again, louder, more audible this time. On his third attempt, she stopped.

Lena froze. For a moment she was too scared to turn around.

When she did turn, her tears blinded her from seeing clearly the tall figure rushing to her.

Rubbing her face with the palms of her hands, desperately trying to stem the flow of tears, she didn't give him a chance to have a go at her for her rudeness when he reached her, saying in a tearful rush, 'I'm so sorry, I didn't mean to skip out without saying goodbye.'

'Then why did you?' he asked with surprising gentleness.

'Why do you *think*?' she wailed, rubbing away more tears. 'I thought I could do it, okay? But like with everything else, I was wrong. I didn't know it would hurt so much. I'm sorry if I've embarrassed you and I'm really sorry if I've hurt your parents' feelings. I promise I'll apologise in person in the morning, just, please… I need to be alone. Please, Tinos, go back to your family. I'm fine.'

'Lena…'

'Just *go*,' she cried, losing all control. 'Please, Tinos, I can't see you. Don't you get that? It's just too soon. I should never have come here.'

Without waiting for a response, she stumbled off, barely able to put one foot in front of the other. They didn't want to cooperate. The whole of her body was screaming at her to turn back to him.

'Lena, you're not the one who needs to apologise.' There was a tremor in his voice that made her feet refuse to take another step. 'That's on me. It's all on me. I'm the one who should be sorry. I *am* sorry.'

*Don't turn around*, she pleaded to herself. *Walk away*.

'I've been trying to find the words since you turned up here. I thought I'd imagined you. I did not guess you would come. But I should have. You always do the right thing no matter the personal cost to yourself. It's why your family had to force you to leave your sister and forge a real life for yourself. If they hadn't, you would never have moved to Sweden. It's why you hid the pregnancy from me. You were protecting our baby as best you could despite knowing the longer it took for you to tell me, the angrier and more unreasonable I would be about it, and you knew that anger would be directed at you. It's why you hid your pregnancy from your family, too. You didn't want to add to your parents' worries until it was absolutely necessary or have your sister face the reality of another of her dreams never being realised. You always put everyone else's needs above your own.'

She heard the crunch of his footstep closing the small gap she'd created. When he next spoke, his voice was so close she could feel it breeze against her hair.

'You came here today for my family's sake. You knew you would see me. You knew it would hurt you, and still you came. For their sake. Strangers to you. If I wasn't already in love with you, that would have pushed me over the edge into it.'

Her breath caught in her throat.

She swayed as air swirled around her, and then hands rested gently on the tops of her arms. 'Please, Lena, look at me.'

For the first time since that one glance on the terrace all those hours ago, her eyes overrode her will and met his stare.

What she found there sent ripples through her heart. It was the same agony she knew was mirrored in her own eyes.

'I'm truly sorry, Lena. For everything. I'm sorry

for my cruel proposal. I'm sorry for being a gutless coward. All these years I've let my brother's betrayal fester in me. Infect me. It cut too deep for me to realise his betrayal had actually done me a favour.'

He must have read the question in her eyes for the smallest smile pulled on his lips. 'I never loved Cassia. Not really. I loved the idea of her. I'd spent so many years infatuated with her that when we got together, I thought I had to be in love with her. If I hadn't met you, I might have spent the rest of my life believing it.'

He lifted his hand and brushed his fingers over her cheekbones. She felt them tremble against her skin.

'But I did meet you. And my heart recognised you. I have fought it every inch of the way and I have hurt you. That kills me. My blindness. I pushed you away in the most cowardly way and it was deliberate. Deep down I knew you would never agree to that insulting proposal, and all I can say is if you give me another chance, I swear on our child's life that I will never push you away again. Not ever. I love you, Lena. I want to spend the rest of my life with you. You're the sun who lights my entire world and I can't go on without you.'

From spending the entire day avoiding his stare, Lena now found herself unable to tear her gaze from his. She didn't want to, anyway, not when such sincere, heartfelt emotion was contained in the green depths.

'Give me your hand,' he whispered.

It gave itself to him willingly.

He held it tightly to his chest. 'Do you feel that?' he asked in that same barely audible voice.

The strong beats of his heart thumped against her palm.

'This is yours to do with as you will. My heart and my life are entirely in your hands.'

Her own heart swelled like a balloon to fill every crevice in her chest, pumping blood that fizzed through veins that had feared they would never feel joy again. The fizz seeped into her skin and bones until every cell in her body was suffused with the warmth that came only from Tinos, and suddenly she could contain it no more. She was never certain if she threw her arms around his neck or if her arms threw themselves, but around his neck they went and all the agony they'd both lived in their time apart healed in the passionate urgency of their fused mouths.

Breaking apart, they stared at each other in wonder.

'I love you,' he said, his words sweeter than manuka honey.

'I love you more.'

'Not possible.'

Cupping her face in his hands, he pressed his forehead to hers. 'You will marry me, won't you?'

Lena laughed. She couldn't help it. 'Just try to stop me.'

A beaming smile broke out on the face she loved with all her heart and then he was squeezing her tightly, overwhelming relief pouring out as laughter from his mouth and into her hair, and as their dizzying happiness soared in the air like a cloud around them, their baby woke up and had a party in Lena's belly to celebrate.

# EPILOGUE

STARS FILLED THE skies over Trollarudden. Lena, absorbed with the Christmas present her darling husband had gifted her with, stared through the powerful lens in rapture and astonishment. The *colours* she could see up there were...

'Hot chocolate?'

Moving her face away from the telescope, she beamed at Tinos and tilted her head for a kiss.

With a vampiric grin, he obliged, his green eyes flashing when he pulled back. She bit back her protest at this kiss, far too fleeting for her liking, when her mother emerged from the back door of the cabin Konstantinos had had rebuilt and extended that summer, carrying a snow-suited Phoebe in her arms. Right behind them came Heidi on her brand-new, all-weather wheelchair, followed by their dad carrying a tray full of mugs of steaming hot chocolate.

While everyone settled on the long bench with Lena, Heidi held her arms out for her niece. It never failed to make Lena's heart melt to see her sister's devotion to the youngest member of their family. Never failed to astound her with the progress Heidi had made this past year.

Lena had believed Heidi's recovery had long ago reached its limit. None of the Weirs had ever thought their beloved Heidi a burden but only once they'd moved into their new, gloriously spacious, wheelchair-friendly home did Heidi confess the guilt she'd felt at all they'd given up for her. Now, with both their parents having resigned their part-time teaching jobs, seeing their mother create pockets of time to fulfil the creative side she'd thought gone forever and their father dig his old golf clubs out of the garage, had lifted Heidi of the guilty burden none of them had known she carried.

But it was Phoebe who'd really proved the impetus for Heidi to throw herself even harder into her physiotherapy and, even with tears streaming down her face from the exertion of it all, strengthen her arms enough to safely hold the niece she was smitten with. Her devotion was entirely mutual and, wrapped in the sanctuary of her husband's loving arms, Lena watched her eight-month-old daughter place a mittened hand to Heidi's cheek with a contentment in her heart she'd never imagined it would be possible to feel.

Konstantinos's phone rang. Placing a kiss to his wife's temple, he disentangled his arms and accepted the video call from Kos.

His clearly inebriated parents filled the screen.

Crowded around them were the rest of his family, and he carried the phone to Heidi and zoomed it in on his pride and joy, his baby daughter. Suddenly, his two nephews barged their way onto the screen to coo at the cousin they were as enamoured by as the rest of the Siopises. A fascinated Phoebe swiped for the phone in return.

Not even the glimpse of his brother in the background could dent Konstantinos's excellent mood. Over the summer they'd made, at Konstantinos's instigation, a rapprochement of sorts. He would never trust his brother and sister-in-law or form any kind of relationship with them outside family gatherings, but his anger and humiliation had evaporated. Lena's steadfast, passionate love had driven it away for good. Let their children be raised as cousins and their parents' loyalties no longer be torn.

Once the call was over, he sat back next to his wife, who was excitedly directing her mother's gaze through the telescope to Jupiter, and reached for her hand.

She leaned into him and tilted her head, smiling widely. 'I love you,' she mouthed.

With his heart as full as it was possible to be but mindful of their audience, he kissed her chastely.

Her fingers squeezed his, the nails digging into his skin a silent signal that when bedtime came, there would be nothing chaste about the kisses they shared.

Laughter filling his chest, Konstantinos cuddled her to him so her head nestled beneath his chin and

his arms were wrapped around her, and stared up
at the stars that could never match the beauty of
the woman he would love and cherish for the rest
of his life.

\* \* \* \* \*

*If you were swept away by the passion of*
Christmas Baby with Her Ultra-Rich Boss
*then you're sure to fall in love with*
*these other Michelle Smart stories!*

Crowning His Kidnapped Princess
Pregnant Innocent Behind the Veil
Rules of Their Royal Wedding Night
Bound by the Italian's "I Do"
Innocent's Wedding Day with the Italian

*Available now!*

### #4153 THE MAID'S PREGNANCY BOMBSHELL
*Cinderella Sisters for Billionaires*
by Lynne Graham
Shy hotel maid Alana is so desperate to clear a family debt that when she discovers Greek tycoon Ares urgently needs a wife, she blurts out a scandalous suggestion: *she'll* become his convenient bride. But as chemistry blazes between them, she has an announcement that will inconveniently disrupt his well-ordered world... She's having his baby!

### #4154 A BILLION-DOLLAR HEIR FOR CHRISTMAS
by Caitlin Crews
When Tiago Villela discovers Lillie Merton is expecting, a wedding is nonnegotiable. To protect the Villela billions, his child must be legitimate. But his plan for a purely pragmatic arrangement is soon threatened by a dangerously insatiable desire...

### #4155 A CHRISTMAS CONSEQUENCE FOR THE GREEK
*Heirs to a Greek Empire*
by Lucy King
Booking billionaire Zander's birthday is a triumph for caterer Mia. And the hottest thing on the menu? A scorching one-night stand! But a month later, he can't be reached. Mia finally ambushes him at work to reveal she's pregnant! He insists she move in with him, but this Christmas she wants all or nothing!

### #4156 MISTAKEN AS HIS ROYAL BRIDE
*Princess Brides for Royal Brothers*
by Abby Green
Maddi hadn't fully considered the implications of posing as her secret half sister. *Or* that King Aristedes would demand she continue the pretense as his intended bride. Immersing herself in the royal life she was denied growing up is as compelling as it is daunting. But so is the thrill of Aristedes's smoldering gaze...

HPCNMRA1023

## #4157 VIRGIN'S STOLEN NIGHTS WITH THE BOSS
*Heirs to the Romero Empire*
### by Carol Marinelli

Polo player Elias rarely spares a glance for his staff, until he meets stable hand and former heiress Carmen. And their attraction is irresistible! Elias knows he'll give the innocent all the pleasure she could want, but that's it. Unless their passion can unlock a connection much harder to walk away from...

## #4158 CROWNED FOR THE KING'S SECRET
*Behind the Palace Doors...*
### by Kali Anthony

One year ago, her spine-tingling night with exiled king Sandro left Victoria pregnant and alone. Lied to by the palace, she believed he wanted nothing to do with them. So Sandro turning up on her doorstep—ready to claim her, his heir and his kingdom—is astounding!

## #4159 HIS INNOCENT UNWRAPPED IN ICELAND
### by Jackie Ashenden

Orion North wants Isla's company...and her! So when the opportunity to claim both at the convenient altar arises, he takes it. But with tragedy in his past, even their passion may not be enough to melt the ice encasing his heart...

## #4160 THE CONVENIENT COSENTINO WIFE
### by Jane Porter

Clare Redmond retreated from the world, pregnant and grieving her fiancé's death, never expecting to see his ice-cold brother, Rocco, again. She's stunned when the man who always avoided her storms back into her life, demanding they wed to give her son the life a Cosentino deserves!

---

**YOU CAN FIND MORE INFORMATION ON UPCOMING HARLEQUIN TITLES, FREE EXCERPTS AND MORE AT HARLEQUIN.COM.**

HPCNMRB1023

# Get 3 FREE REWARDS!

**We'll send you 2 FREE Books plus a FREE Mystery Gift.**

**FREE** Value Over **$20**

Both the **Harlequin® Desire** and **Harlequin Presents®** series feature compelling novels filled with passion, sensuality and intriguing scandals.

---

**YES!** Please send me 2 FREE novels from the Harlequin Desire or Harlequin Presents series and my FREE gift (gift is worth about $10 retail). After receiving them, if I don't wish to receive any more books, I can return the shipping statement marked "cancel." If I don't cancel, I will receive 6 brand-new Harlequin Presents Larger-Print books every month and be billed just $6.30 each in the U.S. or $6.49 each in Canada, a savings of at least 10% off the cover price, or 3 Harlequin Desire books (2-in-1 story editions) every month and be billed just $7.83 each in the U.S. or $8.43 each in Canada, a savings of at least 12% off the cover price. It's quite a bargain! Shipping and handling is just 50¢ per book in the U.S. and $1.25 per book in Canada.* I understand that accepting the 2 free books and gift places me under no obligation to buy anything. I can always return a shipment and cancel at any time by calling the number below. The free books and gift are mine to keep no matter what I decide.

Choose one:  ☐ **Harlequin Desire**        ☐ **Harlequin**          ☐ **Or Try Both!**
                   (225/326 BPA GRNA)          **Presents**              (225/326 & 176/376
                                               **Larger-Print**           BPA GRQP)
                                               (176/376 BPA GRNA)

Name (please print)

Address                                                                          Apt. #

City                              State/Province                       Zip/Postal Code

**Email:** Please check this box ☐ if you would like to receive newsletters and promotional emails from Harlequin Enterprises ULC and its affiliates. You can unsubscribe anytime.

---

Mail to the **Harlequin Reader Service:**
**IN U.S.A.:** P.O. Box 1341, Buffalo, NY 14240-8531
**IN CANADA:** P.O. Box 603, Fort Erie, Ontario L2A 5X3

**Want to try 2 free books from another series! Call 1-800-873-8635 or visit www.ReaderService.com.**

---

*Terms and prices subject to change without notice. Prices do not include sales taxes, which will be charged (if applicable) based on your state or country of residence. Canadian residents will be charged applicable taxes. Offer not valid in Quebec. This offer is limited to one order per household. Books received may not be as shown. Not valid for current subscribers to the Harlequin Presents or Harlequin Desire series. All orders subject to approval. Credit or debit balances in a customer's account(s) may be offset by any other outstanding balance owed by or to the customer. Please allow 4 to 6 weeks for delivery. Offer available while quantities last.

**Your Privacy**—Your information is being collected by Harlequin Enterprises ULC, operating as Harlequin Reader Service. For a complete summary of the information we collect, how we use this information and to whom it is disclosed, please visit our privacy notice located at corporate.harlequin.com/privacy-notice. From time to time we may also exchange your personal information with reputable third parties. If you wish to opt out of this sharing of your personal information, please visit readerservice.com/consumerschoice or call 1-800-873-8635. **Notice to California Residents**—Under California law, you have specific rights to control and access your data. For more information on these rights and how to exercise them, visit corporate.harlequin.com/california-privacy.

HDHP23

# HARLEQUIN
## PLUS

Try the best multimedia subscription service for romance readers like you!

---

## Read, Watch and Play.

Experience the easiest way to get the romance content you crave.

Start your **FREE TRIAL** at
<u>www.harlequinplus.com/freetrial</u>.